MINI-BIKE

Racer

DISCARDED

CLAIRE MACKAY

Cover by
Brian Boyd

Scholastic Canada Ltd.

Scholastic Canada Ltd.
123 Newkirk Road, Richmond Hill, Ontario, Canada L4C 3G5

Scholastic Inc.
730 Broadway, New York, NY 10003, USA

Ashton Scholastic Limited
Private Bag 1, Penrose, Auckland, New Zealand

Ashton Scholastic Pty Limited
PO Box 579, Gosford, NSW 2250, Australia

Scholastic Publications Ltd.
Holly Walk, Leamington Spa, Warwickshire CV32 4LS, England

Illustrations by Merle Smith.

Canadian Cataloguing in Publication Data

Mackay, Claire, 1930-
    Mini-bike racer

Rev. ed.
ISBN 0-590-73637-X

I. Title.

PS8575.K27M56 1991   jC813'.54   C91-093440-1
PZ7.M32Mini 1991

10 9 8 7 6 5   Printed in Canada   1 2 3 4 5/9
Manufactured by Webcom Limited

To Gerald Ransom, who asked me to write this book.

Chapter 1

Steve scratched and scratched and scratched. His cast was off. Finally. He looked with distaste at his left arm, free at last of its plaster cocoon. It was wrinkled, flaky and white. With his right hand, already brown from the June sun, he scratched again, hard. Well, a few days out on the trail with his mini-bike would fix it up. He walked out to the hospital waiting room.

"All ready, son?" Tall, dark-haired John MacPherson dropped an ancient *National Geographic* into the magazine rack and stood up. "Feel up to going out to Lost Mountain for the race?"

"You mean . . . to ride, Dad?"

"Of course not. You need at least a week or so to get that arm in shape. No, I just thought you might want to watch Kim win another ribbon."

Steve laughed a little ruefully at the teasing. In the past month the Queensville Mini-Bike Club had sponsored two race meets, but Steve had ridden in neither of them. Although he had begged to try one-armed, his parents' refusal had been unbending. No amount of pleading had moved them: he had been condemned to sit on the sidelines and watch his best friend, Kim Chambers, ride off with top honours.

"Sure, Dad, I'd like to go." His mouth set determinedly. "I'll be in the next race, though, no matter what! After all, without me we wouldn't even have a club, right?"

"That's right, Steve." His father dropped a fond arm across Steve's shoulders for a moment. "Seems a long time ago, doesn't it?"

"Sure does," answered the boy, remembering. His May adventure did seem years instead of weeks ago: that marvellous day in Antler Hills with Pete Sikorsky, his mechanic friend; Pete's accident as a sudden spring storm caught them on the muddy slope; his own desperate efforts to save the church camp from the rampaging Pronghorn River; and then that wild nightmare ride through the forest to find the Mounties, when Steve had lost hope, consciousness and the use of his arm before he reached their headquarters.

But the nightmare had been worth it. His dad had become a real mini-bike fan, and together with Kim's father and Pete Sikorsky, he had organized the Mini-Bike Club, which now boasted thirty members. Steve shook his head in wonder — it was hard to believe everything had turned out so well. In the dark days of last February, when his father wouldn't even let him mention the word mini-bike, he would never have believed that five months later they would be going to a bike race together. Zow! It really freaked him out.

* * * * * * * *

They eased into the crowded parking lot, slowing and swerving for the goggled riders on their way to the starting line. It was a quarter to two. In fifteen minutes the major event of the meet, the senior race, would begin. The Peewees had been run at eleven that morning; the Powder Puff, for girls only, at noon. All the specials — the "roadeo," the slaloms, the obstacle and wheelie tests — had long since been judged. There remained only the cross-country for twelve-year-olds and up, the climax of the day.

Steve left his dad at the awards table talking to Al Chambers and Mr. Pinkerton, the town alderman, and wandered over to the track in search of Kim. He found him bent down by his bike, fiddling with the chain.

"Hi, Kim! Bike okay?"

Kim looked up. "Hi, Steve. Got your cast off, huh?" He paused. "Yeah, the bike's okay. But you know me, I get nervous before every race." He glanced at his watch, a frown developing between his brows. "They should be blowing the whistle to line up . . . "

As if in answer, a sound, shrill and commanding, slashed through the hubbub like a razor. Hunched at the starting line in a walking cast, Pete Sikorsky, chief mechanic, referee, peace officer and ardent fan of all the riders, had blasted the signal.

"Thar he blows!" said Steve. "Good luck, Kim! You'll win, no sweat! Just wish I was out there with you!"

"Yeah? That's one thing *I* can do without," laughed Kim as he hurried his machine to the track.

Steve stared after him. There had been a hard edge to Kim's laugh that Steve found new and disturbing. He wondered about it for a moment, then shrugged. Kim was probably just uptight about the race.

At the crack of the starter's pistol, the mini-bikes were off in a rain of gravel and dust. Standing with his father and Mr. Chambers, Steve watched through binoculars as Kim grabbed the lead. It was really no contest — the other riders, three girls and eight boys, were trailing by fifteen metres as Kim disappeared over the first hill.

An hour later the story was the same. Popping up on the crest of the ridge, face stained with dirt, boots mud-splashed, Kim was honking along all alone. Another red ribbon to add to his collection, Steve thought enviously. He hurried down to the finish line as Kim roared in, with Julie Brennan, a girl from Murdoch Corners, flashing by close behind him with a reckless

4

last-minute spurt that brought applause from the spectators.

Mr. Pinkerton, sweating, heaved his well-fed bulk up the steps to the awards table and waved for silence.

"Ladies and gentlemen, boys and girls," he began, "it gives me great pleasure . . . " Steve's mind wandered. He had heard Mr. Pinkerton before; it usually took him quite a while to get to the point. Then, startled, he heard his own name.

"Is that Steve MacPherson over there? Steve, come on up here. I think you should do the honours — it's only right after all. Glad to see your arm's better.

"Now, ladies and gentlemen, boys and girls, I'm sure all of you remember what Steve did last April. He was a real hero!"

Oh, no! Steve squirmed with embarrassment, his face hot as fire. He felt like a fool!

"Saved a whole village out by Antelope Run, Steve did. Yes, sir! Been nominated by the town council to go all the way to Ottawa to get a medal for bravery. And he deserves it. Yes, sir!"

Steve, agonized, looked over the heads of the crowd at a point far, far away and wished he were there. He groaned inwardly.

At last Mr. Pinkerton was running down. "So here, Steve, you pass out the ribbons today. Next race I bet *you'll* be the winner. Yes, sir."

Flushed, his mind a welter of confused feelings, Steve

somehow managed to get through the next few minutes. Handing Kim the first-place ribbon, all scarlet and golden glory, he tried to catch his eye. But Kim stood before him stolidly, avoiding his gaze, his mouth a thin unsmiling line.

Chapter 2

Steve hurried over to Kim, who was wiping down the frame of his bike. He had to smooth things over. That stupid Pinkerton! All that garbage about the flood. Man, he should get a ribbon too — for being a first-class idiot! *Yes, sir!*

Steve was suddenly nervous, and his voice shook a little as he said, "Way to go, Kim!" He gave his friend a gentle slap on the back. Was it his imagination or did Kim stiffen under his touch? "You had it made all the way. No competition, I guess."

Kim did not respond. Steve, uncertain how to proceed, chattered on. "Oh well, now my cast is off I'll really zap you in the next race!" He forced a grin.

Kim straightened up slowly and turned to look at Steve. His eyes flicked to Steve's arm, pale and peeling. But he didn't smile. "Couldn't you arrange to break another arm? I kinda like winning."

Steve's laugh was false, too loud in his own ears, as

he said, "No way!" Trying then to make a joke, trying to melt the icy wall he could almost see forming between them, he blundered on. "After all, you can't expect to beat the hero of Antelope Run, can you? You heard what Pinky said about me, didn't you? Like, wow, man — I am *dy-na-mite!*" He grinned.

Kim's face was expressionless. He swung aboard his bike and rammed it into life. He pulled down his visor, cleared his throat and spat at the ground by Steve's boots. Then he said, above the noise of his motor, "Well, go and explode then!" And he sped away.

As he watched Kim disappear into the crowd, Steve felt as if he'd been kicked in the stomach. Puzzled and hurt, he turned towards the parking lot — and almost collided with Julie Brennan.

Laughing, the girl stumbled backwards. "Hey, MacPherson, watch where you're goin'!"

"Oh! Sorry, Julie! Didn't see you. You okay?"

"Yeah, sure, Steve." She paused. "Uh, I was waiting to talk to you, but if you'd rather not . . . " Her voice trailed off.

Steve glanced at her narrowly. "What do you mean?"

Julie's green eyes dropped before his gaze as she muttered, "Well, it looked like you were just having a fight with Kim. Isn't he supposed to be your best friend?"

Steve grunted. "I thought he was, up until a few minutes ago. Something sure is bugging him." He shook his head, a frown of bewilderment passing over his face. "Talk about cool! Any cooler and he'd be dead. I can't figure it." Steve's voice trembled in spite of himself. He took a deep breath to steady it and changed the subject. "Hey, Julie, you sure looked good coming in. I hear you rode a beautiful race in the Powder Puff too. Sounds like you know most of the tricks."

"That's what I want to talk to you about, Steve. I want to know *all* the tricks. And since you're the best rider around here, I want you to teach me. Next time I'll win more than the Powder Puff." Her mouth curved scornfully. "I don't see why they have a separate race for girls anyway — it's dumb! We don't need special treatment!" Julie's eyes flared with feeling.

"Hey," laughed Steve, "simmer down, kid. You don't have to fight *me* on that — I think it's pretty stupid too. But Mr. Chambers and Pete are kinda old-fashioned. Why don't you ask them to change the rules? From what I saw today, you can ride better than most of the guys." Steve shook his head doubtfully. "I really don't think I can teach you very much. Besides, I haven't been on a bike for six weeks."

"So what? You're still the best." Julie hesitated, then plunged ahead. "I'd like you to come out to my place next Sunday with the Bobcat. We have a stretch of land out near Murdoch Corners, lots of rough ground and a couple of tricky hills out back. Please, Steve?" She stopped for breath.

"Next Sunday? Well, I guess that'll be okay. I don't expect I'll be going any place with Kim." His mouth tightened for a moment. "The Sikorskys are going to Silverbranch that day — maybe they can drop me off. About ten o'clock okay with you?"

"Great! Do you know the Corners? Well, go two or three kilometres past it until you see an old oak beside a dirt road on your right. I'll be under the tree — on my bike." Julie flashed him a grateful smile and turned to go. Then she stopped and turned back again. Laying a hand on Steve's arm, she said softly, "Steve, if you and Kim are friends again by then, bring him along too. Okay?"

"Okay, Julie. Hey, that's really nice of you."

Somehow, as he watched the girl make her way through the parking lot, Steve felt much better.

Chapter 3

As the last days of school wound down like a lazy top, Steve never found an opportunity of speaking to Kim. He was always rushing off somewhere or talking to someone — usually to Nick Adams, the star athlete of Riveredge Public. And a real creep, Steve thought. A couple of times, when there was no way to avoid it, Kim said hello, but his voice was clipped and cold. No longer did they exchange laughing glances, share secret jokes; no longer did they walk in and out of one another's houses. Steve was perplexed and unhappy. He wondered again and again what he had done to cause the break, and what he could do to mend it.

Friday came. There were no classes, only a ten o'clock assembly in the big gym to assign the students their rooms for next year. As Steve's class filed in, he noticed Kim and Nick right behind him, whispering to one another. He glanced away and marched straight ahead, past the first row of folding wooden chairs. Just as he reached a point directly in front of the stage, he felt a hard shove in the middle of his back. He pitched forward and before he could regain his balance a foot appeared out of nowhere to trip him. His arms thrashing, he fell against the girl in front of him, pushing her violently into the boy ahead. In seconds he and seven of his classmates lay in a tangled sprawl on the gym floor while the wooden chairs tumbled and clattered around them.

Steve sprang to his feet and spun around, fists clenched. Kim and Nick, grinning, stood guiltless yards away. He moved towards them, rage rushing through his veins, ready to fight it out.

"Steve!" Mr. Gillespie, the vice-principal, shouted his name in a stern baritone that demanded obedience. Steve stopped and lowered his arms to his sides. He was almost blinded with anger and embarrassment. All around him a pool of silence grew. Everyone was looking at him. Through the quiet he heard Nick's whisper, sharp as a claw. "Man, that character will do anything to get attention!"

For a long moment Steve stood as if carved from marble, hearing his own charged blood beat in his ears. Then he bent to pick up the chairs. The silence broke; a low hum of voices seeped through the room; order was restored.

Except in Steve's furious heart. He resolved to have it out with Kim, once and for all. He heard nothing of the

assembly. Only when the rustles of impatience trailed off, the coughs of boredom ceased, did he realize it was over. He hurried down the hall to his locker and yanked it open. A year of debris perfumed with old sweat greeted him: ragged notebooks; three gym socks; motorcycle magazines; a package of gum, crushed flat by a dumb-bell he had borrowed; a once-white T-shirt, now the colour of old newspaper; his winter boots; two apples, dried and wrinkled like a pair of shrunken heads; an Evel Knievel poster; and one wool glove with the thumb missing. He grabbed his duffle bag from a bent hook and jammed everything into it.

Footsteps sounded on the tile floor. He looked up. Kim and Nick had stopped by the drinking fountain down the hall. Laughing, they sprayed the walls, the floor and each other before swaggering towards him. Steve slammed his locker shut and hurried around the corner to the side door. He wanted to see Kim alone, without Nick. This business was strictly private. Besides, Kim was a different person when Nick was around, cold, hard and mean — a guy Steve didn't recognize.

He half ran out the side door, not caring what they thought. Unlocking his bicycle from the rack, he rode to Ross Avenue and Dominion Street — Kim had to pass that intersection to get home. He hunched down next to his bike and waited, trying to calm the tumult inside him. A few minutes later he saw Kim riding towards him. He was alone.

"Kim!" Steve's voice seemed loud in the quiet street.

Kim slowed to a stop and looked in Steve's direction. He said nothing. Steve could not decipher the expression on his face.

"Okay, Kim, what the heck's the matter with you? Ever since last Saturday's race you've been acting weird. And" — Steve's face darkened with anger — "it was you who pushed me this morning while your pal stuck out his foot, wasn't it?" His throat suddenly tightened and locked, stemming the rush of hot words. He couldn't trust himself to speak.

Kim smiled thinly. "Nick dared me. I never refuse a dare, you know that."

"But, Kim, listen, I still don't get it! Two weeks ago we were" — Steve hesitated, then blurted out — "we were best friends. Or I thought so anyway. Now all of a sudden you're buddy-buddy with Adams and givin' me the big chill. What's wrong?"

Kim looked down at his scuffed track shoes. "Nothin's wrong. You jealous?"

"Of course not!" Steve stopped, afraid to push the conversation into territory he might wish he had never entered. But he couldn't hold back. "And quit lyin'! *Something's* wrong and you know it! And I figure I got a right to hear what it is."

Kim's head snapped up and his eyes bored into Steve's. "All right, you asked for it, MacPherson! You asked for it! I just got more and more bugged with having such a big shot for a friend!"

"Whaddya mean, big shot? Man, if anybody's actin' like a big shot it's Nick Adams. Him and his crummy basketball trophies!"

"You *are* jealous! Just because the only thing you're good at is mini-biking!"

Steve's temper rose like a red mist behind his eyes and his hands curled into fists. He took a deep shuddering breath. He didn't want to fight — he *couldn't* fight with Kim, no matter what. He tried again, his voice trembling with the tension of holding his feelings in check.

"Kim, I'm sorry if it looked like I was throwin' my weight around. I sure didn't — " He got no further. In two strides Kim was beside him, his angry face just centimetres away. He hadn't heard a word.

"You think you're so great, don't you? Ever since you got your picture in the paper! 'Big hero saves campers'! Boy, nobody ever forgets it! And you don't let them forget it, do you? Bringing your mini-bike to school, hanging around with Mrs. Richards and the rest of the teachers — it was enough to make me throw up! You probably kept the cast on two weeks longer than you had to, just to show off and let everybody know how great you are! And as soon as I start to win a few races, as soon as a few people start to think maybe *Kim Chambers* is somebody, I mean somebody besides Steve

MacPherson's shadow or . . . or his . . . *slave* or something, you show up at the biggest race we've had so far! And what happens? I win the race — yeah, me — *I* win the race. But does anybody notice? How could they? The big hero is with us! With his battle scars and his medals he walks among the peasants! He even stoops to pin the ribbons on the winners! Big deal! Big deal, MacPherson! I've had it up to here with you! I'd sooner have friends who aren't quite so . . . so *famous!*" Kim's mouth twisted, making a mockery of the last word. "And if you try to beat me in the next race, just watch out! I'm out to win, no matter how! I'm gonna *burn* you!"

Steve watched Kim's face in a daze. He could not believe what he was hearing. How could Kim feel this way? And yet . . . he felt a tiny prickle of guilt. He *had* liked the attention, the admiration, the fact that everybody in Queensville knew who he was. Maybe he had liked it too much; maybe to Kim it had looked like an ego-trip.

Kim had stopped shouting. Steve could think of nothing to say. For a full thirty seconds the two boys stood there facing each other. Steve had the strange notion that Kim's words had turned into a cruel sword that had slashed beyond repair the bond of friendship between them, leaving nothing behind it but emptiness. He watched Kim walk towards his bike before he spoke, his voice creaking like a rusty hinge. "All right, Kim, if that's the way you want it."

Kim spun around and barked, "Yeah! That's exactly how I want it! Stay out of my way!"

A sudden blaze of pride and fury almost choked Steve as feeling finally rushed back to him. "Just don't count on winning any more races, old buddy," he shouted as Kim mounted his ten-speed, "because you don't have a chance!" He turned and strode away.

Well, that was over. Done with. Finished. The heck with it. But as Steve rode slowly home, somehow the whole conversation kept returning and returning, like a record stuck in a groove. And unbidden, unwanted, memories returned too, memories of the time when Steve had known a great guy named Kim Chambers.

Chapter 4

"I'll sit in the back with Pete, Mrs. Sikorsky," said Steve as he clambered over the tailgate of the old station wagon. Pete, one leg sealed in the cast which was the last visible reminder of his ordeal that day at Antler Hills, had already settled himself in the back of the wagon and had braced himself against the seats. Pete's wife Anna was driving. The two girls, Lisa and Sophie, squirmed beside her, and before the outskirts of Queensville had disappeared they started to ask, "Are we almost there?"

After a while, Steve started scanning the distance for the big oak Julie had described. He was looking forward to today. It had been a long time — too long — since he'd been out on his mini-bike, and from what Julie had said, this was a great place to ride. It couldn't have come at a better time, he thought . . . then hastily he steered his mind away from the path it was about to follow. Too often lately, unless he kept busy, he found himself going over and over the fight, probing at the wound it had made, probing almost to make it hurt, like picking a scab off a scraped knee. He was grateful when Pete interrupted his gloomy thoughts.

"Well, Steve, you will be ready for the next race, I hope?"

"Sure will, Pete. I can hardly wait!"

"It will be the biggest of the summer," said Pete. "We will hold it at Antler Hills in two weeks, if all things can be arranged. I have talked a little with some friends — mechanics and shop owners in other places — and they have shown great interest." The big man's face creased into a smile. "Riders from as far away as Sheepsneck and Aspen Ridge in Manitoba will come. It is like the races of my youth in the Old Country. We shall have a grand tournament!"

"Hope I'm back in shape by that time, Pete. I'm really out of practice."

Pete clapped the boy on the shoulder. "Hah!" he snorted. "I have no fears — you will win, my boy! Have not I myself taught you how?"

Steve grinned. "I'm gonna try, Pete. I've missed all the fun so far." He paused, lips pressed together and eyes the colour of distant ice. "I guess Kim is the guy to beat — you think so, Pete?"

"He is a good rider, Steve, a good rider. But I do not think you will have difficulty. You are a natural." He looked at the boy beside him. "But something we should think about — your bike can be made better."

"The Bobcat? How, Pete?"

Sikorsky rubbed his mustache. "Well," he said, "for the hill-climb events you will probably need a stronger chain. Also deeper-cut knobbies. A reserve gas tank for the cross-country — it is a good thing to have anyway. And of course everything must be checked — spark plugs, filter, cable. If there is a fault, perhaps your friend Kim will win once more!"

Pete's chuckle died as he saw Steve go pale. The boy looked away and said, "I'm going to win! I'm going to beat Kim! Don't worry about that, Pete!"

Pete searched his young friend's face. It was closed, expressionless. He said no more. It would be better, he decided, to ask questions at another time.

The car radio, up to now a soothing background murmur, suddenly blared in alarm. "We interrupt this program to bring you a special bulletin." The announcer's voice crackled with tension. "Police report a break-out at Elmgrove Correctional Centre. Three men, described as armed and dangerous, made their escape this morning just before daybreak. They are believed to be heading in the direction of Queensville. Police are requesting the co-operation of the public in reporting any suspicious persons or events in the area surrounding the city. To repeat . . . "

Six-year-old Sophie turned to her mother. "Momma, does that mean they're after us?"

"No, no, dear," answered her mother. "They are running away and will not trouble us — they will try to hide from everyone. Don't worry. You are safe." She touched her younger daughter's cheek and smiled.

But Pete was not smiling. His eyebrows pulled together in a worried frown. Steve glanced questioningly at him.

"What's wrong, Pete? You don't think there's any chance we'll see them, do you?"

"Well . . . " Pete shook his head doubtfully. "Maybe not — but we shall be careful on our way home tonight."

"Hey, there's Julie! Mrs. Sikorsky, can you pull over? There's Julie under the tree."

Steve grabbed his helmet and goggles and was out of the station wagon as soon as it stopped. He yanked the Bobcat out of the bumper rack, and with a wave to the Sikorskys, was off.

Chapter 5

"Hi, Steve. Sure glad you could come! Isn't it a super day? Come on up to the house and meet the family. My dad wants to look you over, I think." Julie grinned at him. "Your hair's a bit long — he's sorta square, y'know. Like, would you believe a brush cut?"

Steve laughed along with her. "Don't worry, Julie. I'll say please and thank you and I promise I won't track mud on the carpet. At least not when your dad's lookin' at me!"

Julie led the way on her mini-bike, a neat little 50 cc. Mohawk, bright yellow with royal blue racing stripes on each jaunty fender. They picked their way slowly up the slope of a small hill and stopped at the crest, a hundred metres east of the house. The sound of their engines died away in the silence.

"See out there, Steve? Back by the woods? That's where we can do some real riding!"

"Looks good."

The Mohawk roared into sudden life. "Come on, MacPherson! Race you to the farmhouse!" Swift as a startled fish, Julie sped along the ridge. Steve didn't have a chance — by the time he reached her, she was lounging nonchalantly at the back door.

"Maybe you could teach *me* a few things, Julie." Steve shook his head in admiration. "That was a pretty slick take-off!"

"Yeah, it was, wasn't it?" Julie laughed and beckoned him to follow her into the kitchen where her father, mother, brother and little sister sat at the table. They looked up as Julie and Steve came in. Mr. Brennan rose and shook hands with Steve. He had a brush cut.

"Hi, Steve. Glad to meet you. We saw you at Sunday's race — and of course I guess everyone's heard about your part in the flood last spring."

Steve felt himself getting hot. Would that stupid flood follow him forever? It had already caused him more trouble than he could ever have imagined. Why couldn't everyone just forget it?

"How do you do, Steve?" Mrs. Brennan's voice was low and musical. Steve noticed the auburn tints in her hair, a little darker than Julie's, and the springy copper-coloured curls on two-year-old Kate, who was parading around the kitchen beating on a pot with a big wooden spoon.

"Julie," Mrs. Brennan said over the din, "your dad

and I have to visit Grampa later this afternoon. Could you and Steve look after Kate? We'll only be an hour or two."

"Gee, Mom, why can't Jeff babysit for once?" Julie looked at her older brother with resentment.

" 'Cause I'm working down at the gas station from one till nine — summer hours," Jeff answered. "Sorry, kid, you're it again."

Quickly, to let Julie know he wasn't disappointed, Steve interjected, "That's okay, Julie. I don't mind." He looked at Mr. and Mrs. Brennan. "No girls at our house," he explained. "I've just got two brothers. Sometimes that's two too many!"

The tension eased. Steve, out of the corner of his eye, could see Julie relax and smile along with the others.

"Okay, Mom," she said. "What time do you want us back at the house?"

"About three o'clock," answered her mother. "Thank you, Julie. And Steve." She gave him a grateful look — and a knapsack full of lunch.

Chapter 6

Julie and Steve were sprawled under an ancient elm, finishing off the sandwiches and cookies Mrs. Brennan had packed. It was after one o'clock.

"Well, Julie, you know everything I do. Your speed's good, your handling is great, especially in tight spots, and you've got a lot of guts" — he glanced at her slyly — "for a girl."

Julie snapped upright, eyes flashing. "Steve, you skunk! You're absolutely the last person in the world I thought would make a crummy remark like that! That really bugs me! We were having such a great time and then you . . . "

Steve was rolling on the ground with laughter. Julie looked at him for a moment, and then a sheepish grin spread across her face.

"Okay, okay," she muttered. "That's one for you."

"It's just like pressing a switch," Steve gasped. "Click, and off you go like a giant sparkler!" He sat up and put a hand on her shoulder, suddenly serious. "Really, Julie, I didn't mean it, you know that. As far as I'm concerned you're just . . . just Julie Brennan, a friend of mine. Okay?"

"Okay, Steve," said Julie, mollified. "But sometimes it's a bummer being a girl, y'know, and getting put down for no reason."

"Anyway," Steve went on, "what I was going to say before you exploded was that both of us need practice in trials. Pete wants to have them in the next race, I'm pretty sure."

"You better tell me what they are first. I don't know what you're talking about."

"Well, in a way, trials riding is a race where it's probably more important to be the slowest," answered Steve. "The idea is to ride your bike over a course set out ahead of time in really rough country — rocks and holes and ruts and fallen trees, mud, water, sand, everything you can think of — and never let your feet off the footpegs. If your feet touch the ground, it's called dabbing. Everybody starts with a set number of points, say three or four hundred, and every time you dab, or your hand touches a tree, or you stall or stop, you lose points. The winner is the rider with the most points left. Got it?"

"Yeah, I guess so."

"Want to try it?"

"Sure. Let's go!"

They laid out a miniature course. It led through a series of deep ruts, over three fallen trees whose exposed roots clutched at the air, into a sandy ditch and across a creek bed. Steve noticed a depression on the far side of the creek. He pointed it out to Julie.

"For the grand finale, we'll go through that mudhole there. Now remember: don't sit down, keep your feet on the pegs, never go out of bounds, and keep the engine at a fast idle. Ride as slow as you can without stalling. I'll go first as far as the creek."

Gently, Steve eased the Bobcat into position to cross the ruts. Leaning forward to climb, backwards to descend, he successfully manoeuvred up very close to the first log. Moving his weight cautiously to the rear, he approached at an angle. The front wheel of the little machine rose obediently, touching and grabbing the top of the rough-barked log. He gave it a little more juice, at the same time throwing much of his weight forward on the handgrips. The Bobcat climbed over, neat as a caterpillar.

The two remaining logs were conquered in the same way. Steve began to grin. The rest was going to be a cinch, he thought. He headed down into the ditch, reached the sandy bottom — and suddenly felt his balance going. Too late he remembered the first commandment for riding on sand: speed. And as the bike teetered, his left foot, reacting instinctively, stamped down hard on the treacherous earth. Glancing up, he saw a wicked grin on Julie's face. He gritted his teeth, and sizing up the bank of the ditch, made a quick judgement. He gave the Bobcat a reckless dose of gas and in less than a second had reached the top.

"Okay, Julie, your turn!" he shouted. Julie pulled on her gloves and refastened her helmet. He watched as she rode through the obstacles he had just crossed, hesitant, awkward at first with the rapid weight shifts. But she kept her balance, her feet firm on the footpegs as if stuck with glue. Down into the sandy ditch she went, her face intent and serious, and up the other side — without a spill. She braked to a stop beside Steve.

"Oh, wow, Steve, that was hard work! I never thought going slow could be so tough."

"Beautiful, Julie, just beautiful! What's more, you beat me." Steve shook his head in mock bewilderment. "How come?"

"Well, I'll tell ya, my friend . . . I'm just naturally great!"

"You sure are!"

"Never mind, Steve. You did all right . . . for a boy!"

Steve's eyes widened. Then he grinned and said, "Okay, we're even. Now, are you ready for the creek? Of course, in a real trials we wouldn't have stopped — we'd have gone straight through the whole course."

He squinted at the shallow water ahead. The bed of the creek looked safe enough — no rocks, no branches, no current. Steve decided to take a straight run at it. Riding well back on the Bobcat, he gave it a good shot of juice and aquaplaned neatly across. The muddy depression was slightly to his right. He veered towards it — and knew, too late, that he had guessed wrong about how deep the hole was. The Bobcat's front wheel lurched down into the slippery mud. And so did he. He turned his head to warn Julie but there was no time. She was hurtling towards him at full clip, water skimming up behind her like a peacock's tail. He had time only to see her shaken face as, trying to avoid him, she yanked her bike to the left, skidded wildly — and landed right beside him in the muck.

In the sudden quiet, broken only by a low gurgle as Steve sank still farther, they sat blinking at each other. Then the corners of Julie's mouth quivered and she scooped up a glove full of mud and pitched it right at Steve's head before collapsing, choked with giggles, backwards into the slime. Steve, the muck dribbling off his chin, was silent for a moment. Then he said, straight-faced, "You know, Julie, I don't think we did that right."

Chapter 7

Julie's parents had gone. Steve, fresh from a shower, smiled at Kate as he finished checking the carbs and plugs on the hosed-down bikes.

"Ready to go, kid?" he asked.

Kate's eyes lit up like twin traffic lights. "Go!" she squealed.

Steve sat Kate in front of him on the Bobcat, his helmet askew on her red curls, and slowly followed Julie towards the line of elms half a kilometre to the rear of the farmhouse. A wooden swing, worn smooth by countless Brennan bottoms, hung lazily from the lower branches of the tallest tree. Kate headed straight for it.

"Push, push," she demanded of Steve. Steve pushed. And pushed. He might have pushed the whole afternoon if Julie hadn't diverted Kate to a nearby sandpile. Using an old tin can, a spoon and an unfettered imagination, the two-year-old happily got into the castle business.

The afternoon was sleepy, peaceful. Julie and Steve,

their backs warmed by the summer sun, lay on their stomachs and talked contentedly. Soon Steve felt his eyes drooping shut.

Suddenly he woke with a start, his heart pelting like hail on a tin roof. Julie was shaking him.

"Steve! Steve, wake up! Kate's gone!"

Steve was on his feet in an instant. He ran to the sandbox with Julie at his heels.

"Kate!" he shouted. "Kate, where are you?" Together they ran through the grove, calling her name.

"Steve, where could she be? We've got to find her! It's my fault, it's all my fault!"

"Okay, Julie, okay! We'll find her — she can't be far. Let's go back and get our bikes. We can cover more ground riding."

Astride her machine, the engine running, Julie shouted, "I'm going back to check the house. She might have gone there. Look through the trees again and wait for me."

Steve did as he was told. Within a few minutes Julie was back. Her face, drawn with worry, answered his unspoken question.

Grimly they set out, thirty metres apart, criss-crossing the rough country where earlier they had ridden so lightheartedly. Nothing. Steve lifted his eyes and surveyed the distance with a long sweeping glance. The afternoon sun made him squint. He pulled down his goggles to cut the glare. What was that? Something had moved near the crest of the first rise, where they had started their trials test. There it was again — a bobbing cap of curly hair was disappearing over the hill.

"Julie, look! Up there!" Steve pointed. "Let's go!"

Recklessly they spurred their bikes forward, abandoning caution for the sake of speed. Steve reached the top of the incline first. He looked about wildly — Kate had vanished! He cut his engine and in the sudden hush breathed a deep sigh as he heard the child's welcome babble nearby. But underneath her voice was another sound, strange and ominous — an ugly sound that made Steve's skin twitch. Julie came swooshing up beside him and killed the Mohawk's engine. Then two pairs of eyes widened in dismay.

A few metres away, Kate jabbered away to a dog — or was it a wolf? — whose leg was caught in the clenched metal jaws of a trap. The animal growled, its lips a fierce dark ring around bared teeth, its neck and back muscles rippling under angry fur. Unaware of the danger, Kate kept repeating "Here, doggie," as she toddled closer and closer on her fat unsteady legs.

Steve gave Julie's arm a brief touch, warning her not to move, then kicked the starter and raced towards the child.

The metres seemed an endless distance. Steve felt as if he were travelling in slow motion. He saw Kate's plump fingers reach out, saw the fearful glisten of the dog's slashing teeth . . . If ever he had to be perfect in his approach and his timing it was now.

The sudden appearance of the Bobcat startled both the child and the dog. For one split second they were frozen — the split second that Steve needed. Heedless of the uncertain terrain, he curved the bike in towards Kate, and held out his good right arm. The Bobcat wavered under the impact as he caught her, and he heard her stifled gasp of protest. Then, mercifully, they flashed out of range of the frantic animal.

Chapter 8

Kate was unimpressed by Steve's gallantry. Red-faced, she screamed with rage and squirmed like an octopus. "Doggie! Doggie!" she yelled. "Down, Steve, down!"

"Oh, Kate! We thought you were lost!" Julie's voice shook with relief. She wiped the tears from her eyes and held out her arms to her baby sister.

Steve glanced over at the trapped dog; it was quieter now, but every minute or two it snarled defensively.

"Why the trap, Julie?"

"To catch whatever killed two of our best hens last week. Dad thought it might be a wolf, though nobody's seen one around here for thirty years. Or a dog gone wild." She nodded in the direction of the growling animal. "Maybe that's him."

"That's not a killer dog! For one thing, wild dogs are too smart to walk into a trap. And he's hardly more than a pup, a year old at the most. He's probably a stray." Steve studied the animal again, a quick sympathy stirring within him. "Julie, lend me your scarf for a minute."

Julie's eyebrows lifted uncertainly, but she shrugged and untied the kerchief, passing it to Steve's outstretched hand. Dismounting from the Bobcat, the boy began to approach the dog with cautious steps. The animal watched him warily, sniffing the air. When he was a few metres away, Steve started to talk in low crooning tones. "It's all right, boy, it's all right. You're a good dog. It's all right . . . " The growling stopped; the dog's ears cocked forward and the tail moved slightly. Steve could see the markings now; the dog was a German shepherd pup. The almond-shaped eyes, bright with intelligence, looked up at him. Steve imagined he saw a plea in them before the dog lowered his head once more to push vainly at the cruel jaws which gripped his right forepaw.

Steve knelt and swiftly wrapped Julie's scarf around the dog's long nose to make an efficient, if make-shift, muzzle. The dog tried to snarl, but his locked mouth could form no more than a piteous whimper. Still murmuring to him, Steve clasped his paw just above where it was caught. Then with a sharp thrust he brought his booted foot down on the extended flat spring. The trap loosened, the teeth unclenched and the jaws fell loosely to the ground. Steve lifted the dog free.

Julie, still clutching Kate, had come closer to watch. Steve held up a restraining hand. "Keep Kate away till I have a look at this paw. The dog's pretty nervous."

With gentle fingers, Steve kneaded the leg below the first joint. The dog didn't jump or pull away. The paw was swollen and dried blood marked the matted area where the jaws had clamped shut, but nothing seemed broken. Probably just a bad bruise, Steve thought. He let go of the paw. The dog stood up and tried his weight — and promptly sat down again and cried.

Steve sat down with him. Whispering encouragement, rubbing the silky ears, he undid the scarf. "There you go, pup. Go on, now. Go home. Find your way home."

The dog put his head on one side and whimpered.

"Where's he supposed to go?" asked Julie. "You said yourself he's probably a stray. And I'm sure he doesn't belong around here — we'd have heard if anyone had lost him." She looked at the dog and started to smile. "I think you just got yourself a dog, Steve."

As if understanding her words, the pup leaned over and licked Steve's face from chin to forehead. Steve turned and looked at him. All at once he wanted the dog. Very much.

He stood up, walked several paces away, then turned around.

"Here, boy! Here, boy! Come on!" He slapped his thigh in encouragement. The pup looked at him for a few seconds, then tried to get up. The front paw gave way. Trembling, the dog sat down again.

"Come on, boy!" Steve called again, a note of

38

entreaty creeping into his voice.

The dog wagged his tail until dust rose up like a mist around him. He stood, wavering, with his weight on three legs. Then, lurching forward, he stumbled to the place where Steve stood waiting.

His eyes suddenly wet, Steve knelt down and threw his arms around the dog's neck. He looked at Julie and broke into a shaky grin. "I guess you're right, Julie. I just got myself a dog."

Chapter 9

"Hey, Pete," yelled Steve from the back door of the Cycle Shop. "Where are you?"

A muffled voice answered from somewhere beneath the floorboards. "Down here. Wait — I will come up." A trap door pushed upwards in a little alcove off the main workroom, and Pete Sikorsky heaved himself into view. His weathered face glowed with pleasure. "Ah, you have come, Steve," he said. Then, with a puzzled look, he glanced beyond the boy to the door. "But where is Jake?"

Ever since Steve had adopted Jake as his own, they had been inseparable. Where Steve went, Jake went too. Queensville had quickly grown accustomed to the sight of the boy and the dog. The bond between them was almost visible.

"Julie took him to the park," Steve replied. "They're going to meet me here at eight." He looked at his watch. "That only gives us half an hour to work on the

Bobcat. Think we can get much done in that time?"

"Oh sure, Steve," answered the big mechanic. "I have already done the big jobs. We can make a good start on what is left to do, then I can finish tomorrow. But tonight is Friday — I keep the shop open till nine. We might be interrupted." He shrugged. "So, we will not let that stop us. Come and give me some help."

Together they heaved the little bike up onto the long, low worktable, removed the wheel assemblies and made certain all the air was out of the tires. Once both wheels were apart, they began to take off the shallow-cut tires, using small irons made especially for minis.

"One moment, Steve," said Pete. "Let's try heavier ones. I have some somewhere." He went to the back of the workroom and poked through a maze of bike parts, tools and tires. "Ah, here's a pair on a Trail 70 that was traded in last week."

The bell over the front door tinkled faintly. Pete muttered something short and explosive and put down his wrench. "Can you get these wheels off, Steve? I will be back as soon as I can."

Steve laboured in silence, repeating on the Honda the step-by-step routine he had just learned on the Bobcat. Soon both wheels were side by side on the floor, but Pete had still not returned. Steve walked to the curtain which hung between the workroom and the shop — and froze.

Pete was standing behind the counter, his eyebrows

forming an angry line across his face. Confronting him was a monstrous apparition: a man with a stocking pulled over his head, warping the flesh of his face into a grotesque mask. In his hand he held a gun. And he was aiming the barrel directly at Pete's chest.

"All right, old man," said the figure, "for the last time, hand over the cash! Quick!" The gun flicked.

Pete didn't move. He was not a man to surrender what belonged to him without a fight. His mouth was taut, his muscles tense.

Neither man had yet noticed Steve, who suddenly remembered the pay phone at the corner by the jewellery store. If he could just get out the rear door . . . Carefully he dropped the curtain and took a step backward. Carefully he started to turn — then his foot touched a wheel and it clattered to the floor! The robber whirled. With one bound he reached the doorway, yanked the curtain aside and grabbed Steve by the hair, pulling him against his own body, back into the shop. At the same moment, Pete snatched a gun from a narrow shelf below the counter.

Steve could smell the man's sweat, could feel the hollow thrust of his heartbeat, could see through his unbuttoned denim shirt the medallion that lay on his chest, an enormous carved cobra's head of hammered silver with two red stones for eyes.

"Old man, don't try anything," the robber hissed when he saw Pete's gun, "or the boy gets it."

Steve felt his hair wrenched to its roots as the criminal pulled him closer. The pain forced tears to his eyes. But he could still see, far too clearly, the tobacco-stained fingers that tightened on the butt of the pistol.

Chapter 10

As if in a dream, the three figures stood unmoving. Far away, the library clock slowly tolled eight.

Finally Pete set the gun on the counter. "Let the boy go. I will get the money."

Steve felt himself released. His knees sagged suddenly and he leaned against the counter for support. The man snatched up Pete's gun and tucked it under his belt. Then he grabbed the sheaf of bills Pete held out, jamming them inside his shirt.

"That's better, old man. Now don't move. And don't try to call the cops." Abruptly he lifted his gun and fired. The shot was so loud and so close to Steve's ears that he cringed in pain. The telephone behind Pete burst into bits of black plastic which showered to the floor. "That should slow you down," the thief grunted. Then with two oddly lurching strides he was out the door.

Pete came around the counter as fast as his cumbersome cast would let him. "Steve, are you all right?" He put his hands on the boy's shoulders.

Steve looked up at his friend. "Pete, I'm sorry. I was trying to get out the back to the phone booth, but that ape saw me first."

"You are sorry, Steve?" Pete's voice trembled. "I am glad only that you came to no harm. If he had hurt you . . . But now you must go and call the police. Just dial the operator and she will give you the station. Tell them to come right over." He sighed tiredly. "I will make us some strong tea, I think."

Steve ran to the phone booth on the corner. He had just finished delivering his message when down the street he saw Julie and Jake crossing towards the shop, unaware that anything had happened.

Suddenly, with screeching tires, a car rounded the corner from the back lane and flashed past him. Julie was directly in its path! Numb with surprise and fear, staring in bewilderment at the onrushing car, she stood holding Jake's leash, unable to move. She was going to be hit! A terrible anguish rose in Steve's throat. As the car gathered speed, he yelled with all his strength, "Julie! Jake! Move!"

His alarm shattered Julie's trance; she started towards the sidewalk. And Jake, hearing his master's voice, strained against the leash, tugging her along. They just made it. The right fender barely missed Julie as the car raced down the road, spitting gravel like buckshot. Blinded, she fell to the ground while Jake, pulling free, galloped after the speeding car.

Steve dashed to Julie's side. "Julie! You okay?"

Julie sat up slowly, her eyes dazed. She swallowed convulsively, then whispered, "Yeah, I think so. What kind of screwball was that?"

"That was probably the thief who just robbed Pete. You should've seen him! I just called the police . . . " Helping Julie to her feet, Steve poured out the details, not even stopping when Jake came bounding back, his leash dragging. Absently he patted the dog's head, picked up the leash and followed Julie into the shop. Inside, Pete paced in silent anger as Julie told him about the car.

Within minutes, two police officers had arrived. "How much did he get away with, Mr. Sikorsky?" asked the younger constable after Pete had told his story.

Pete swallowed a huge gulp of tea before he answered. "Counting the cheques, it would be nearly five hundred dollars." His mouth hardened.

The constable whistled softly. "That should keep him going for a few days," he muttered. "He'll throw away the cheques, though — if he's the one we have in mind."

Pete eyed the young policeman curiously. "And who is this thief you have in mind?"

"Well, Mr. Sikorsky," the older officer replied, "maybe you heard about the Elmgrove break a week ago Sunday?" Pete nodded. "Two of the men have been

46

recaptured, but the third is still at large. His name is Claude Mallory, and this is his kind of stick-up. It's the same sort of crime that got him sent away in the first place. He started ten years ago, when he was sixteen, and he's never changed. He hits small shops with only one clerk — variety stores, gas stations, all-night restaurants, that kind of thing. Mallory's violent and unpredictable — and very dangerous." The corporal drew a deep breath. "We'd like to get him before someone gets hurt."

He turned to Steve. "Now, Steve, what can you add? Tell us everything you can, even if you don't think it's important."

"Well, he had this stocking mask over his face, so I don't really know what he looked like." Steve paused. "But one thing I did notice — he was wearing a medallion around his neck. Silver. It was a snake's head with rubies for eyes. Oh yeah, and something else. I think there was something wrong with his foot or leg. When he ran out the door he was sort of off balance."

The policemen exchanged a swift glance. "That's Mallory, all right," said the younger one. "Steve, you've been a great help." He snapped his notebook shut.

"Hey, wait!" Steve exclaimed. "Nobody told you about the car. I saw it when I was coming back from the phone booth. It came out of the lane goin' eighty, I bet, and headed north on Dominion Street." He looked at Julie, then at the two listening police officers. "He almost hit Julie."

"Did you see the licence plate? The model? Colour?"

"It was a four-door sedan, dark, a Ford, I think. Saskatchewan plates. I'm sorry, but I didn't notice the numbers."

"I saw the last three," Julie announced. "They were two, one, one. That's all I saw, though, before Jake pulled me out of the way . . . "

"That's terrific!" the corporal said. "Mr. Sikorsky, I'd appreciate it if you, Steve and Julie would come down to the station tomorrow to make statements." He turned to his partner. "Come on, Jim — looks like we've got work to do."

Pete walked with the two men to the front door, then carefully locked up, throwing the bolt shut with stern vigour. Steve poured out three mugs of tea and quietly handed one of them to each of his friends. They sat without speaking for a few moments, side by side on the workroom bench.

Finally Pete spoke. "Well, you two, it's almost nine. You'd better be getting home."

"Yeah, I guess so." Steve looked at the big man slumped beside him. "You okay, Pete?" he asked anxiously.

"I'm okay, Steve. I will work a little on the Bobcat and then go home. If you can come tomorrow morning, we will finish it up. Then Julie can meet us here at lunch time and my wife will take us down to the police station." He sighed noisily through his mustache. "Steve, let us hope that you and I have no more adventures for a while. I grow too old for the excitement that has happened since we met each other." He smiled at the boy.

Steve grinned back. "I'm aging fast myself, Pete," he said. "All I want now is a nice peaceful summer. Besides," he added to Julie as they went out the door with Jake, "what else could possibly happen?"

Chapter 11

Sergeant Buckler sighed. "No, Steve, there's no sign of him."

"Do you think he went north?" asked Julie, looking at the huge map of Saskatchewan stretched across one wall of the office at the Queensville police station. The map was dotted with push pins, making the provincial crime statistics vivid and colourful. Six green pins stood as mute symbols of the smash-and-grab robberies of Claude Mallory.

Bill Buckler came from behind his cluttered desk to join them. He was tired. The Mallory case had been assigned to him right after the prison break two weeks ago, and he hadn't slept much since. His mouth tasted like a drainage ditch from too much coffee and too many cigarettes.

He jabbed a long forefinger at the topmost green pin, a hundred kilometres northeast of Queensville. "You mean because of this? The stick-up at Tailfeather

Lake? Yeah, maybe you're right." He rubbed his red-rimmed eyes. "But we're not even sure yet if that was Mallory."

Steve, Julie and Pete had just finished a detailed recital of the robbery. A constable in the outer office was now typing up their statements. Julie and Steve were eager to be on their way: tomorrow was the big race, and Mrs. Sikorsky had promised to drop them off at Julie's for one last workout. The Bobcat was snugly tied to the back of the station wagon parked out front. Jake was standing guard.

"I heard on the radio he was heading for the States," said Julie.

"Julie," the big detective sighed, mashing out his nineteenth cigarette of the day in disgust, "as soon as we posted the reward, everybody saw Mallory everywhere! In the past forty-eight hours he's been spotted in Toronto, Calgary, Detroit and Yellowknife!"

The telephone rang. Shaking his head in exasperation, the sergeant lifted the receiver. "Buckler here . . . Okay . . . Bring 'em in . . . Thanks." He hung up. "Your statements are ready to sign. After that you can go."

Minutes later the three friends walked towards the front door, accompanied by the detective. Just as they stepped into the entrance hall, Buckler was hailed by a small dark young man. Steve looked at him closely; he seemed familiar. Then he remembered. It was Wally

Devlin from the *Gazette,* Queensville's evening paper. He was a good reporter — or maybe just a stubborn one. From Steve's father — who could do a pretty fair imitation of a stone statue — Devlin had somehow managed to extract the full story of the Antler Hills flood last spring and had given it front-page treatment with five-centimetre headlines.

"Come on!" Steve whispered to Julie and Pete. "Let's get out of here!"

"What's the big rush? What are you whispering for?"

"I'll tell you outside. Come on!"

They hurried through the doorway and down the cement steps as fast as Pete's cast would permit. Jake had already scented them; his tail wagged exuberantly.

"That's the newspaper guy who covered the flood. I don't want him to — " Steve's voice faltered. Behind him, Devlin called his name.

"Steve! Steve MacPherson!"

And in front of him, just coming out of Sullivan's Sporting Goods, Nick Adams and Kim Chambers turned to stare.

As Devlin ran up, Jake growled menacingly. His neck fur rose and his tail stuck out like a starched banner. Steve laid his hand on the dog's head and said, "It's okay, Jake. He's a friend. Sort of." Jake relaxed.

Nick and Kim lounged against a nearby car, hands in the back pockets of their faded jeans. A toothpick bristled at one corner of Nick's mouth. They watched as Devlin whipped a notebook out from inside his jacket and checked the camera swinging from his shoulder.

Nick yelled, "Hey, Kim, is that MacPherson kid in the news again? My, oh my, what has that wonderful boy done now?"

Anger flashed through Steve. He clenched his hands to keep them at his sides. " . . . So that's the story, Mr. Devlin. Anyway, we all gave our statements to Sergeant Buckler. You better talk to him. Okay?" Without waiting for an answer, Steve turned to follow Pete, who was already heaving himself into the station wagon.

"Hey, MacPherson, you the big hero again?" Nick's voice cut through the Saturday afternoon hubbub.

Steve said nothing. His jaw muscles ached with strain. In the silence he heard Kim's faint murmur.

"Hey, Nick, take it easy. Let's go. We've got better things to do." He put his hand on Nick's arm but the other boy shook him off in annoyance.

"Hey, MacPherson, I hear there's a big mini-bike race tomorrow."

"What's it to you, Adams?" Julie broke in.

"I also hear that Kim is gonna wipe everybody, especially the big-shot hero. That right?"

Julie exploded. "You are really out of it, Adams, you gimp! Steve is gonna win. And if he doesn't, I will." She glanced scornfully at Kim. "Your flunkey there hasn't

53

got a chance. So why don't you go — go catch a basketball in your mouth! It's sure as heck big enough!" She swung towards the wagon and opened the back door with a vicious twist. "Come on, Steve. The air's too polluted around here!"

Steve looked at Kim. He hadn't moved. His face was scarlet and the corners of his mouth trembled. Steve felt the hard and heavy space inside him lighten. He took a quick step in Kim's direction.

But the moment of opportunity — if there had been one — vanished in the next second. Nick grabbed Kim's arm and snarled, "You're right, man! We've got better things to do! Let's head out!"

Steve got into the wagon beside Julie, with Jake at his feet. As they pulled away he glanced back. Kim was watching him with a strange expression in his eyes.

Soon they reached the Brennan oak tree. In a matter of moments the Bobcat was unloaded and the Sikorskys were ready to go.

"Thanks a lot, Pete . . . Mrs. Sikorsky," Steve said. "See you tomorrow at the race."

As the station wagon pulled away, Steve turned again to look at the Bobcat. "What do you think, Julie? Pretty neat, huh?"

"Wow, Steve, it looks terrific! You and Pete really did a job on it!"

"Yeah. Looks really mean, doesn't it?"

A sorcerer with a wrench, Pete had transformed the

little bike. New spoked wheels with knobbies that would grip the earth like claws now rolled proudly under the emerald fenders; the cylinder had been bored to take a larger piston ring; along one side, to further increase the thrust, hung an expansion chamber; and a reserve gas tank rested snugly in front of the original.

"Pete says it'll put out close to five horsepower now." Steve smiled, then his blue eyes turned hard as agates. "Man, I'm gonna wipe that Chambers!" His jaw was a stubborn square. "So come on, kid — we've gotta practise." He turned and whistled for Jake. The dog abandoned the intoxicating smell of a gopher hole and bounded over the rugged slope, skidding the last two metres to tumble at Steve's feet.

Julie picked up her bike at the house and the three companions set out, Jake running in a long easy stride alongside the bikes. No matter how many hills they climbed, creeks they forded, woods they ranged, fields they crossed, the dog was right beside them — or ahead of them, waiting. Finally Julie called a halt. She pulled to a stop at the crest of the hill overlooking Murdoch Corners and pushed up her visor. Jake, his tongue hanging out, sat back on his haunches as Steve shut off the Bobcat and swung off to stretch his legs.

After a moment Julie joined him on the rough grass. Talking now and then of tomorrow's race, they rested there, dreaming in the afternoon sun.

Chapter 12

Steve jumped out of bed and pulled the drapes open. Sunlight flowed through the window. A perfect day for the race! His nerves tightened and excitement rose in him like a fountain as he thought of what the coming hours would bring. He had a hunch, an exultant hunch, that he would win.

He opened the closet door and dragged out a long cardboard box which read, in large script, *SULLIVAN'S SPORTING GOODS*. A surprise from his dad. After the weekly shopping on Thursday night, his father had asked him to unload the trunk of the car. When all the parcels were in the kitchen, his dad had pointed to the box and said, "Open it, Steve. It's for you. For the B average on your report card. Never thought I'd see the day!" And then he had said, "It's really just something I wanted you to have." Remembering, Steve smiled. His dad was okay.

He took the lid off the box and looked with renewed

delight at its contents: gloves, boots and a set of racing leathers. What a sight! The leathers were split grain, navy blue, with parallel stripes of crimson and white down the outer side of each leg. They fitted him like a second skin. Plastic caps covered the knee areas, and around the hips was an extra layer of padding. He would be able to bail out at top speed and never get a scratch! And they looked so great, Steve thought, as he pulled them on. With the new long gauntlet gloves and the full bore boots, he'd be just like a real pro. For the jumps he had a wide kidney belt, and newly attached to the scarred helmet, once worn by Pete in European championship races, was a wrap-around visor made of safety plastic. With this outfit, with the Bobcat souped up and with his own soaring confidence, nothing — and no one — could stop him! Kim Chambers might just as well stay home!

Jake bounded into the room and sniffed suspiciously at the new pants. Steve looked down and grinned. "How do you like them, boy? Smell like something to eat?"

He grabbed Jake's nose affectionately, then wrestled the dog to the floor. Joyously Jake entered into the play, snapping, growling, pretending to nip at Steve's hands and feet. Each time Jake struggled upright, Steve would sweep his back legs out from under him and Jake would fall on his rump in an undignified huddle. Finally, breathless with laughing, Steve stopped. Jake wagged his tail and licked his master's ear. Panting, they lay for a few minutes, side by side on the floor.

Then Steve jumped to his feet. "Come on, Jake. It's a big day. We've gotta get movin'!"

Two hours later, John MacPherson, Steve and Jake drew into a makeshift parking lot in a clearing in the Antler Hills area, three kilometres north of the highway. Above them hung an enormous cloth banner announcing the tournament.

Everywhere was noise and confusion. Antler Hills had never seen anything like it. Shouts from excited young throats and the roar of 50 cc. engines made a musical thunder in Steve's ears.

He unloaded the Bobcat from the rear rack. There was lots of time yet. The races would begin at ten o'clock, but the first events were for junior riders aged nine and under. To give the older riders something to do, Steve's dad and Pete had set up a few one-heat motocross races, or "scrambles," open to all contestants.

Mr. MacPherson had gone at once to join Pete. Steve could see them beside the judges' platform, a rough structure of planks and cement blocks. They stood with their heads together, clutching clipboards and comparing notes, each wearing a white armband with "Race Marshal" on it. Just then Al Chambers appeared with a suitcase. Unlocking it, he piled the trophies and ribbons on the platform. Each trophy was a tiny silver mini-bike on a mahogany base, with a small shield where the winner's name would be inscribed. The sun glinted off them, half-blinding Steve as he stared at them. Finally, out of the case came the Grand Award, the prize for the highest scorer in the tournament — a tall gold statuette of a racer, intent, daring and triumphant, bent low over a sleek, streamlined bike.

Steve looked at it. "That's going to be mine," he whispered to Jake. "Tonight that's going to be mine!" Then he noticed Kim standing at the other side of the platform, gazing fixedly at the golden racer. Kim's head turned, as if he felt Steve's glance. Their eyes locked. Across the space that separated them, a silent challenge was flung.

Then Pete Sikorsky, whistle to his lips, stepped onto the platform and pierced the morning air with a blast that made the hills ring. The tournament had begun.

Chapter 13

The one o'clock sun beat down relentlessly on Steve's helmeted head as he eased the Bobcat into a deep gash in the earth. For over an hour the seniors had been riding trials, and of the eighteen riders who had started, only twelve remained. Steve was pretty sure Kim was still in — he had caught a glimpse of him a few minutes before, his face tight with effort as he worked his way across a treacherous outcrop of shale — and ahead of him he could see Julie's chestnut hair. But he had no idea who was winning.

So far, he had managed six clean sections: no dabs, no stalls, no veering out of bounds. There were two sections yet to negotiate before he reached the red handkerchief that was tied to a stick on the rise a hundred metres north of him. Immediately ahead was the next challenge, a dry, crusted creek bed layered with pebbles. It looked easy, but Steve knew that if he started to skid it would be like riding on ball bearings. The trick was to skim over at just the right speed.

"Come on, baby," he whispered as the Bobcat responded to his touch. Good! The purr of the motor, the hum of the new knobbies, the rush of air against his face — everything felt right. The complex rhythms of the machine and of his body meshed in a perfect pattern of movement.

He looked up for a second to see how far he had to go before decelerating. Ahead of him he spotted the bright yellow and blue of the Mohawk, canted dangerously to the left as Julie strained to stay vertical. "Oh, no!" he said aloud, and tensed to the right in unconscious sympathy.

It helped neither of them. Julie was forced to use her foot to prevent a spill, and Steve had ruined his own equilibrium. Desperately, he fought to remain upright, but it was too late. His right boot fell off the footpeg and scraped the slippery stones beneath. Out of the corner of his eye he saw his father, who was judging this section, shake his head and mark something down in his notebook.

"Well, there's five points gone," Steve muttered in disgust. With an effort, he thrust the thought from his mind. The last section was just metres away. It was a hill-climb, and at the top fluttered the red pennant. But before he could reach it he had to thread his way through a series of curves as tight as a coiled spring.

Steve took a deep breath. Carefully he spurred the

Bobcat into the first curve, bending his body slightly to the right. Then quickly to the left, and back to the right again. The big danger was stalling. Too much brake and not enough gas on one of those turns and the motor would die underneath him. His energies gathered and focused to drive him upward in a dizzying spiral.

Barely two metres away hung the red flag. Steve lifted his eyes to it briefly, then flashed by. He had finished the course.

He stopped and took off his helmet. Sweat poured down his face and neck; his T-shirt clung to his back like adhesive tape. Parking the Bobcat, Steve walked towards the shade of a nearby poplar. After two strides, his knees began to quiver. The accumulated tension of ninety minutes of trials riding caught up with him and he sank gratefully to the ground. Nothing could ever be so hard again.

Almost instantly he was startled by a thumping and crashing behind him. Jake was charging through the clumps of scrubby undergrowth, overjoyed at finding Steve again. He licked the boy's face from ear to ear, his pink tongue like an eraser rubbing out the smudges of dirt, while Steve, laughing, tried to fend him off.

"Hey, Steve!" It was Julie, strolling towards him on foot. "Did you do okay?"

Steve grimaced. "Dabbed once in the creek bed," he said disgustedly.

"Yeah, so did I. That was a cruel run, huh? Glad it's

over," she sighed, sitting down beside him. "Hey, look, here comes Kim."

Steve's eyes followed hers as Kim came bobbing over the hill, his face striped with dirt and sweat, his eyes and mouth narrowed with concentration. Passing the scarlet marker, he straightened up and relaxed in the saddle. Knowing so well how Kim felt, wanting to share the experience as he would have in the old days, Steve felt a pang of sorrow. Abruptly he turned away.

"We'd better get down to the platform. They'll be announcing the winners any minute. Kim was the last to come in."

With Jake padding along beside them, they pushed their way through the cars and bikes and kids and parents to the platform where Al Chambers, John MacPherson and Pete Sikorsky stood scanning the score sheets and notebooks.

Steve tried a little mental arithmetic: Kim had won the scramble that morning and one of the three heats of the motocross. Steve had won two heats and taken first place in the quickie flat track Pete had improvised on the plateau. Which meant that . . .

"Ladies and gentlemen, boys and girls!" Kim's father's voice boomed into Steve's thoughts. "As you know, all the awards will be given out at the end of the day. But just to keep you on the edge of your seats, here are the leaders in the senior class so far. Now nothing's final, let me make that clear. We still have the big race at three o'clock. But" — Steve bit his lip. Mr. Chambers was squeezing every last ounce of drama out of this — "so far the leading contenders are . . . in third place, from Aspen Ridge, Manitoba: Andy Kubylak, with four hundred and fifty-three points!"

There was a round of applause, with a couple of cheers from the Manitoba crowd. Steve noticed Kim standing near the parking lot, listening intently.

"In second place, from Murdoch Corners, with four hundred and seventy-seven points: Julie Brennan!"

The clapping was long and loud, punctuated with ear-splitting whistles. Steve threw an arm around Julie and hugged her. "Way to go! That's great!" Julie smiled at him happily.

Mr. Chambers waited until the last faint echo of applause had lost itself in the distant hills before he continued. "And with four hundred and eighty-one points, from Queensville" — he stopped, smiled at the crowd, then yelled — "tied for first place: Kim Chambers and Steve MacPherson!"

Steve stood motionless, alone in his thoughts. The applause, the cheers, the whistles seemed to reach him from far away. Slowly he turned to meet Kim's eyes as Kim began to walk towards him. In a moment they stood face to face.

"Steve, I'd like to wish you good luck in the cross-country." Kim's voice was toneless.

Steve swallowed. When he was sure he could speak,

he said, "The same to you, Kim." He stuck out his hand. "Shake?"

Kim hesitated a fraction of a second before he gripped Steve's hand. Then he turned and walked quickly into the crowd.

For what seemed a long time, Steve just stood there. Then finally he said, "Come on, you guys. Let's go eat."

Chapter 14

"Julie! Hey, Julie!"

Keeping one hand on Jake's collar, Julie turned around to see who was calling her.

"Oh, hi, Mr. MacPherson. Is Steve back yet?"

"I don't know. I was just going to ask you the same question. It's almost time for the cross-country." He frowned at his watch and then at the wild hills beyond the river. "Did he tell you where he was going?"

"No, he didn't. He just asked me to look after Jake for a while. Said something about a funny sound in the Bobcat he wanted to check out."

"Not like him, not like him at all," the man muttered, half to himself. He drew a deep breath as a whistle shrilled. "That's Pete giving the fifteen-minute signal, Julie. You'd better get ready." He reached for the dog. "Here, I'll tie Jake up." He started to lead the animal away, then turned back as if suddenly remembering something. "Oh, by the way, Julie, good luck."

"Thanks, Mr. MacPherson," Julie answered. But now worry had infected her too. The wonderful excitement that had been building within her at the prospect of the cross-country vanished like steam. She tried to make light of it. Steve was okay, she told herself; he was an experienced rider. But what if something had gone wrong with the Bobcat? . . . Well, he had a repair kit with him. He'd probably come roaring in at the last minute. It was silly to worry!

Then all at once she remembered that her dad had warned her about a treacherous slope a few kilometres north, where the overhangs along the steep bank seemed innocently firm until you stepped on them. Steve could have . . . Fear gripped Julie's mind. No! Not Steve! She fought down her alarm and hurried towards the Brennan truck.

Glancing over at the awards platform, Julie saw that the riders were beginning to line up. Race numbers had been issued and now hung from each machine's handlebars. Quickly she gassed up from the can in the back of the truck and checked the cable, chain, brakes and ignition. Then she pulled on her white leathers, gloves and wrap-around helmet and walked the Mohawk to the starting line.

Kim drew up beside her. He was silent for a moment as he scanned the group of riders surrounding them. He looked at his watch, lifted his visor and asked, "Where's Steve?"

Julie almost told him to get lost, but the look on his face stopped her. Instead she said, "Wish I knew, Kim." Shading her eyes against the sun, she stared at the western hills. "He went back towards the Pronghorn River. Said he had a few bugs to work out of the Bobcat." She looked back to the platform. The marshals had gathered. "They're gonna blow that whistle any sec. If he's late, he'll be disqualified." She glanced at Kim. "I suppose you're glad. You'll probably win now." Then bitterly she added, "But Steve could ride circles around you any day!"

Kim said nothing. He swung off his bike, kicked the stand out to support it, and walked over to his father. In a few minutes he was back. Julie looked at him curiously.

"I asked them to delay the start for ten minutes," he said. "I'm sure Steve'll show up. He just wouldn't miss this race!" He paused. "Unless something happened . . . "

Julie reached over and touched Kim's arm with her gloved hand. "Hey, Kim," she said softly, "that was nice of you."

The boy flushed a little and muttered, "Steve would've done the same for me."

Side by side they waited. Up on the stand, John MacPherson spoke low and earnestly to Pete, whose brows knit together as he peered at the hills. Suddenly Pete walked to the front of the platform, impatiently swinging his cast.

"Ladies and gentlemen, boys and girls," he bellowed. Julie chuckled. Pete sure didn't need a megaphone. "There will be a slight delay in starting the forty kilometre cross-country race. One of the contestants has not yet arrived. We shall wait for" — the big man looked at his gold pocket watch — "for ten minutes, until three-fifteen. I know you are all eager to begin. Please try to be patient. I shall blow the whistle twice when I wish you to come to the starting line."

The burly mechanic stepped down awkwardly from the stand and conferred for some time with Steve's father and Al Chambers. Finally Julie saw them nodding as if they had come to a decision. She left the Mohawk and walked over to where they stood.

"Mr. MacPherson, what are you going to do? Why don't you call off the race?"

"No, Julie, we can't do that. Too many kids have come too far. We'll go ahead with it. But I'm setting out now with a couple of the other men to have a look. If we don't find him" — he took a deep breath — "then we'll drive down to the Mountie headquarters at Antelope Run and get a search party organized." He tried to smile as he looked down at the girl beside him. "Now don't worry, Julie. He's probably on his way back right now. He'll have heard the engines revving up. Likely his watch stopped or something." Julie smiled back. But she knew that neither of them was fooling the other.

Pete came stomping over. Very softly he said, "I cannot delay any longer, John. We must start the race. I am sorry, as sorry as you are, I believe." He gripped the other man's shoulder for an instant, then turned back to the platform.

Two minutes later the white flag in Pete's hand flashed earthward.

Chapter 15

Steve pulled to a stop and killed the engine with a quick jab. The sputtering cough he had detected earlier had now vanished. The Bobcat was healthy again — all she had needed was a good run in the open country to clear her out. Satisfied, Steve got off the little machine and stretched his cramped muscles.

It was country he had not seen before. He was standing on a slight rise of land about three kilometres north of the Pronghorn, by his calculations about five or six kilometres beyond the tournament grounds. He looked at his watch. Ten after two. Got a few minutes yet, he sighed, as he sat down and loosened his bootlaces.

Steve still didn't know how he really felt about the race. Sure, it'd be great to win, to hear the crowds cheer, to tuck that golden statue under his arm and walk away. But he knew that a lot more than the trophy was at stake. It could mean the final unhappy break with Kim. Maybe he should throw the race, make a stupid mistake or pretend that something was wrong with his bike. Then Kim would win — which he sure wanted to do.

But if he threw the race it wouldn't be fair to anybody, especially Kim. Besides, he could never get away with it. Kim was too smart. He'd be suspicious right away if Steve said he had had engine trouble, or if he unloaded in tricky terrain. And then, if Kim won, it wouldn't mean anything to him. To throw the race would be an insult, a real put-down. Steve decided that he couldn't do that to Kim — or to himself. He would ride the best race he could, no matter what.

But afterwards, he thought, remembering the handshake and the wish for good luck less than an hour ago, he would go to Kim and try to patch things up. Somehow he was sure everything would work out all right. Suddenly he felt better than he had for weeks.

As he started to heave himself up, Steve noticed a series of small ridges between his feet. They were too uniform to be natural, too even and patterned. They looked like the marks of a tire tread, but they weren't made by his bike. But how could a car have driven in here? It was nearly impassable country, a tough ride even for a mini-bike. Then he remembered: Pete had told him there had once been a road back here when the old dam was being built — a road that might still permit the passage of a car.

Curiously Steve followed the tracks. Five metres, ten,

fifteen — then the trail simply disappeared. Ahead was a thick wall of bush. No sign of a car, or a truck, or anything. Tentatively he reached out to one of the bushes. It came away in his hand. He pulled again. A huge bundle of saplings and willow brush fell to the ground, revealing a dark green fender.

Steve's heart pounded. Moving towards the rear of the car, he swept the branches away from the licence plate. The red numbers leaped up at him. *Five, six, three . . . two, one, one.* Stunned, Steve stood still for a full half minute. Then, bursting with the energy of fear, he scooped up the fallen branches to hide the car once more. He had to get out of here, get word to the police! He turned to go — and stopped short.

In front of him a silver cobra swung hypnotically, its blood-red eyes glowing in the sun.

Chapter 16

Transfixed like a butterfly on the end of a pin, Steve gazed at the medallion.

"Well, hi there, kid," said Mallory in the rasping whisper Steve had not been able to forget. "Nice of you to drop by. Real nice of you. I think you just might come in handy!"

With a sudden vicious jerk, he twisted Steve's arm behind his back and forced it up towards his neck. Steve gasped with shock, certain his wrist was about to break again.

"March, kid!"

Gritting his teeth against the pain, Steve marched. Beyond the wall of brush which had concealed the car stood a broken-down shack. The roof, swept by years of wind and rain, was open to the sky in three places; the small window was a rough and empty square; the front door, held by one rusty hinge, teetered backwards on a fallen beam.

"Keep goin'!" Mallory emphasized his command by shoving Steve into the cabin. When his eyes had adjusted to the murky light, Steve could see a bunk built into one corner. A stretched canvas sheet hung from it in stained shreds and two blankets, soiled and rumpled, lay on the floor at its foot. Across from the bunk stood an ancient iron stove, its rusty pipe running to a hole in the wall. On a rickety table in the centre of the room sat an open can of beans, a bottle of whiskey and a small transistor radio. Leaning against the far wall was a semi-automatic rifle.

Mallory pushed Steve across the room, then fumbled around under the bunk, muttering to himself. Finally he pulled out a short piece of dirty, heavy rope, and standing Steve against the wooden upright of the bunk, passed it around the post and over the boy's wrists, yanking it so tight it bit into his flesh and numbed his fingers.

His task finished, Mallory grunted and turned away. Picking up the bottle of whiskey, he kicked the only chair in the room closer to Steve, sat down and stared at the boy in silence. Then he unscrewed the cap of the bottle and took a long swallow.

"What's your name, kid?"

"Steve."

"Steve, eh? Mine's Claude. Claude Mallory. Last time we met I didn't introduce myself, did I?" He swallowed another mouthful. "You'll have to excuse me,

Steve, if I don't offer you a drink. Don't wanna break the law, y'know." He laughed, a series of short, sharp barks. From under lowered lids, Steve watched him warily. The hairs on the back of his neck shivered.

"Did they talk about me on TV?"

Steve was stunned. The question was so unexpected, the tone so pleading and childish, that for a moment he was struck dumb.

The moment was too long for Mallory. Lunging forward, he grabbed one of Steve's ears. Pulling it cruelly, he shouted, "Did they talk about me on TV?"

Tears rushed into Steve's eyes. His ear felt as if it were being twisted right off. Finally he managed a shaky reply: "Yes."

Mallory's face curved abruptly into a smile. He released Steve's ear. "Well now, whaddya think of that? What'd they say? Did they have a picture of me? I sure hope it wasn't one they took in the slammer! Tell me about it, Steve, and don't leave nothin' out." He moved his chair closer.

Steve recited everything he could remember from the newscast, and when he ran out of facts, switched to fiction. Anything to keep Mallory happy.

"Yeah, the whole country knows about you now, Claude," Steve said. Mallory's eyes were alight with pride. "The announcer talked about how you were arrested for armed robbery when you were only sixteen." He faked a look of admiration.

Mallory's mouth twisted. "I wouldn'ta been caught if it hadn't been for my chicken partner," he growled.

Steve hurried to say something else. "And he said the police don't know where you are."

"Yeah?" Mallory grinned with pleasure. "Don't know where to start lookin', eh?" He spat on the floor. "Stupid fuzz."

"Yeah," agreed Steve. "They figure you headed south to Montana."

Mallory stood up so suddenly the chair toppled over backwards. He kicked it across the room, his face dark and mottled with anger. Grabbing Steve by the front of his racing jacket, he shouted, "And that's where I shoulda been, that's where I woulda been if that crummy car hadn't packed up on me." Saliva spattered like rain in Steve's face.

Then, abruptly, Mallory's tone changed to silk once more. "But I'll get there, Steve, I'll get there," he said, relaxing his grip, "because you, Stevie baby, are my ticket. Did you know that?" He put his face next to Steve's and growled, "You're my ticket outa this crummy place!"

"What — what do you mean?" Steve, choked by the fumes of whiskey, could hardly get the words out.

"Well, they'll be lookin' for you soon, won't they? From the race, I mean." Mallory snorted with laughter. "Oh, yeah, I know what's goin' on. Big mini-bike race the other side of the Pronghorn, right? You ain't there,

and you should be there. So they'll send out a search party, right? And when they get here" — Mallory's teeth bared in a tobacco-stained grin — "they're gonna have to pay my price if they want you back."

Giving Steve a final shake that left his head ringing, he mumbled, "I'm not goin' back to do heavy time. Never. They'll have to kill me first!" An odd look came into his eyes — a look that Steve had seen some other time, some other place. The memory teased him, then abruptly vanished as Mallory's fist tightened on the leather of his jacket. "But before they do that, I'll kill *you,* Stevie baby!"

Chapter 17

"Twelve kilometres," Kim whispered, the words making a thin mist on his plastic visor. Another twenty-eight to go — over the roughest country he had ever travelled.

Pete Sikorsky, holding up a hastily-sketched map, had explained the course to the waiting boys and girls a few minutes before the white flag had dropped. From the awards platform they would ride to the wooden bridge at the forks of the Pronghorn River. At that point they were to check in with Mr. Chambers, who had set out ahead of them on Pete's big BSA. Then they would return by a different and longer route, along the winding riverbank and across a deeply gullied stretch of land marked with dense undergrowth and rocky outcroppings. The run from the platform to the bridge was almost eighteen kilometres, from the bridge back to the platform just over twenty-two. At each kilometre stood a red flag with the number printed on it. It was the twelfth of these Kim had just passed.

Whew! He swerved quickly to avoid a boulder that had thrust up magically from the earth in front of him. Part of the course was an old Indian trapping trail, much of it traversing wild country. Almost from the start Kim had discovered that a constant speed was impossible — in some sections he had been forced to creep along at five kilometres. But whatever his speed, five kilometres or thirty-five, the course demanded a steady alertness.

Number fourteen. He glanced behind him. As far as he could see, he was all alone in front, leading the pack. No sign of Julie. For the first eight kilometres she had been tailing him, a strong second, but on a clear stretch just after the tenth flag his more powerful machine had roared ahead. Now she was nowhere in sight.

He would win. He knew it. That golden trophy would be in his bedroom tonight. The vision warmed him. But the vision faded and the warmth died as the thought he had tried to smother once again surged to the surface: Where was Steve? *Where was Steve?* The words echoed in his mind until he could have sworn they were spoken aloud.

Steve should be in the race. It just didn't feel right without him. Steve should be riding beside him. Or, Kim reflected wryly, more likely in front of him. Steve would have won this race. So big deal; what was winning? Suddenly Kim didn't care about the trophy. He remembered the great times he and Steve had shared earlier in the spring, when both their bikes were brand-new. Where *was* he?

Fifteen. Kim's eyes swept past the red marker. Why, *why* did they have that stupid fight? Kim knew it had been mostly his fault and he had felt like kicking himself a million times ever since. Sure, Steve's getting all the attention had bugged him. But he should've kept his cool, not made everything worse by going along with Nick's crummy trick in assembly and forcing the fight with Steve afterwards. Ever since, he'd had no choice but to hang around with Adams, the top jock in the school. He was a great basketball player, no doubt about it. He was a terrific runner too. But he was a lousy friend. All he thought about was how to look good to other people. It was one long ego-trip all the time and Kim was pretty sick of it. A friend was somebody you could laugh and share jokes with, or talk seriously to — somebody you cared about, and who cared about you. Somebody like Steve.

Where was he? What had happened to him? Had he been in an accident, thrown off his bike by some hidden crevice in the trail? Had he crashed into a lurking tree root or a jagged rock grown over with moss? Was Steve lying bruised and blood-covered in some lonely ravine beyond the river? Terrible images rushed in at Kim and fear clutched his belly.

He glanced ahead. The bridge was just down the next hill. But what was that to the northwest? A slender spiral of sooty air curled skyward. Smoke! A grass fire, maybe, or a careless camper. Or could it be a signal? Hope rose in Kim's throat. It might be Steve!

The bridge was only metres away as Kim spurred his bike forward. On a stump at the far end of the bridge sat his father, smiling to see that his son was the first rider to appear. For a fleeting moment Kim was sorry it had to work out this way, but then he was on the planks and barrelling towards the other end. As he raced by his father, he shouted, "Dad, I'm leaving the race! I've gotta find Steve!"

He saw astonishment dissolve his father's smile. For an instant regret flared. Then he muttered, "The heck with the trophy! I've got to find Steve!"

Chapter 18

Julie glanced over her shoulder as she sped past marker thirty-five. The Kubylak kid was coming up fast; the big black *17* on his handlebars was getting clearer and clearer as he narrowed the gap. Angry with herself, Julie shook her head. She had wasted too much time at the bridge talking with Mr. Chambers about Kim's leaving the race. Poor Mr. Chambers was really shook up! Everybody was — first Steve disappearing, then Kim taking out after him. A frown creased her forehead as she thought again of Steve. He had to be okay. He *had* to be.

The growl of the Kubylak bike startled Julie back to the task at hand. But as she flashed by thirty-eight, she smiled to herself. A lot of people were going to get a shock when a girl came roaring across the finish line first! That golden rider would be hers!

Recklessly she spurred the Mohawk forward, rounding an elbow in the trail just metres ahead of the other bike. Braking with her boot, she bent the bike right over on its pipe to get through a concealed jog, then dashed on again. Ahead was a long curving downward slope — and then the finish line! Julie could see the crowd, could see her father waving her on, could see Pete with the beautiful black and white flag raised high in his right hand. With an exultant yell she gave the little Mo its head and swooped down the hill in a cloud of dust. Andy Kubylak was still three bike-lengths away when, almost as in a dream, she heard the checkered flag swish through the air like a whip behind her.

Ten minutes later Julie was holding the trophy with one hand and shaking hands with the other as kids, parents and friends congratulated her. Shouted farewells and cries of "See you next year!" rang through the clearing as the crowd dispersed. The First Annual Prairie Mini-Bike Tournament was over. By the edge of the parking area, Julie caught sight of Steve's father standing by a jeep talking to a uniformed Mountie. Hastily she said goodbye to the last of her well-wishers and ran over to the two men. As Jake leaped up to greet her, she patted his head abstractedly.

"Mr. MacPherson?"

John MacPherson turned and his face brightened as he looked down at her. "Well, Julie, congratulations! You rode a fine race! And you deserve that award you're guarding with your life!"

Julie smiled at the gilt biker she cradled in the crook

of her arm. "Oh, yeah, thanks, Mr. MacPherson. But I wanted to know if Steve has come back yet."

"No, there's no sign of him. But we'll find him. Corporal Edwards" — he nodded towards the Mountie — "has rounded up some troopers and they've already set out. And we've radioed Queensville for a search-and-rescue helicopter. We're going back to the Antler Hills Road to try to reach the Pronghorn. Used to be an old road in there when they built the dam." He glanced down at the dog. "Julie'" he said hesitantly, "I'd like to ask you a favour. Jake here is already nervous and upset and I'm afraid he'd be pretty hard to control in the jeep. Would you look after him for a couple of hours?"

Julie swallowed. It had been on the tip of her tongue to ask if she could come with them to look for Steve.

"Please, Julie? For me?" Mr. MacPherson's voice was low, pleading. "For Steve?"

Julie sighed. "Okay, Mr. MacPherson. Sure. I'll be glad to." She watched the two men as they climbed into the jeep. Her eyes misted suddenly as she said, "And you be sure to bring Steve back with you!"

Jake whimpered and strained after the disappearing vehicle, but Julie held tight to the leash. "Come on, boy, let's go." She led him over to the Brennan truck and put her trophy on the front seat. The parking lot was almost empty. Only the MacPherson Pontiac, Pete Sikorsky's old station wagon and Kim's father's truck remained.

Time dragged as Julie walked Jake around the clearing. "It'll be dark in a couple of hours," she muttered, looking at her watch. Jake seemed as nervous and tense as she was, looking up at her now and then with a glance she could not interpret. Every few metres he murmured low in his throat and sniffed the air. Suddenly, at the far edge of the clearing, he stood absolutely still, nose to the ground, ears pointed forward in stiff triangles.

"What is it, Jake?" The leash went slack as his tail began to twitch back and forth. "What is it, boy?"

Without warning, the dog lunged forward, the sudden thrust of his heavy body catching Julie off guard. Down she sprawled as Jake, frantic, pulled fiercely on the leash. With a snap it flew from her hand and Jake bounded into the bush.

For precious seconds Julie lay there, stunned, gazing at the spot where the dog had disappeared. Then, gathering her wits, she dashed back to the Mohawk, swung aboard and twisted the starter. Moments later she was in hot pursuit.

"Jake!" she shouted above the noise of the motor. "Jake!"

But Jake did not turn, or slow, or stop. He had found what he had been seeking — and he would follow that familiar scent until it led him to his master. Nothing was going to stop him.

Chapter 19

Kim braked to a halt beside a rotting stump. Sloping steeply to his left was the north bank of the Pronghorn River. He looked at his watch. He had been gone three hours, but for some time now he had been moving in circles. And there was still no sign of Steve. At first he had used the plume of smoke as a compass, but he had lost sight of it when he had pushed deeper into the bush; now, although he could see northward for a long way, there was no betraying wisp of grey. The fire, if there had been a fire, was out.

Well, there was no point in hanging around here, Kim decided. It wasn't far back to the clearing where the tournament had been held. He could see a shallow stretch upstream where he'd be able to cross and make his way back. And he might spot Steve's tracks — if he had crossed the river at all, that was a likely place. Besides, Kim was sure his gas was getting low, and he figured his dad would be worried — and mad — by now. He sighed, then brightened a little. Perhaps Steve was already back. Maybe everybody was out looking for him now instead of Steve!

Suddenly Kim noticed something move at the bottom of the slope. The dwindling light played on a shadowy form as it appeared in a clump of willows beside the river. It was an animal of some sort, a wolf or a coyote. Kim narrowed his eyes. Then, as the creature headed for the top of the rise, he recognized Jake. It was Jake! Nose flared, ears pricked, the dog was loping along in an easy purposeful stride. He's caught Steve's scent, thought Kim excitedly. Punching the starter button, he cut across the slope to intercept.

Before he got far, a familiar sputtering made him jump and turn around in the saddle. Julie was racing headlong up the hill on her little Mohawk. What was going on? Quickly Kim skidded down the hill towards the girl and the dog. "Julie! Jake!" he yelled above the roar of his motor.

The tangle of branches and weeds gathered by the leash was slowing Jake down. This gave Kim his chance. Forgetting caution, he gave his machine full throttle to close the gap between himself and the dog. With a final plunging leap, he rode the front tire over the leash, stopping Jake in his tracks and jerking him backwards. Kim jumped off his bike and grabbed the dog's collar as Julie rode up and dismounted.

"Julie, what are you doing here? And Jake?"

"He broke loose," Julie panted. "I was supposed to be looking after him. Everybody's out looking for Steve. And probably for you too. Why did you leave the race, Kim? You could've won!" She stopped, out of breath.

Kim shrugged. "Well . . . I got so worried about Steve that I just took off." He smiled at her. "Besides, why should you complain? You won, didn't you?"

"Well, yeah, I won. But it was hardly fair. You should have," said Julie.

Kim was silent for a moment. Then he said quietly, "No, Julie, Steve should have won."

Jake yelped sharply and they turned to look at him. The dog pulled in despair at his collar until Kim, relenting, let him lead them up the hill and along an old trail. Then he tried to jump forward and suddenly Kim saw why. There, looking as if its owner had just dismounted, was the Bobcat! Kim reached out and touched the engine — cold. From the handlebars dangled Steve's helmet, stuffed with his new riding gloves. Kim stood thinking for a moment, then turned.

"Julie'" he whispered, "come here. There's something weird going on."

Jake pressed forward again, sniffing vigorously along a barely discernible trail. Kim allowed the dog to guide him to a huge clump of bushes. Tail wagging faster and faster, Jake pushed his shoulders and chest through the outer branches, which fell aside as Kim touched them.

"Julie, look!"

For a moment the girl just stared. Finally she stuttered, "K-Kim, that's the car that almost killed me! That's M-Mallory's car!"

Glancing around swiftly, Kim whispered, "Maybe he captured Steve! He must be around here someplace — come on!" The three of them ran down the slope and dived into a clump of thick-leaved bushes. Safely camouflaged, they huddled for several moments without speaking.

Kim broke the silence. "Okay, Julie'" he said quietly, "we'd better make a plan. You stay here with Jake. If he gets too close, he'll bark for sure. I'm goin' up there to scout around. Got a watch?" When the girl nodded, he continued, "Okay. If I'm not back in half an hour, get the heck out of here and find the search party. All right?"

Julie's mouth set in a stubborn line. "I'm coming too. Everybody always tells me to stay behind with the dog. It's not fair! Steve's my friend too!"

"I know, Julie, I know! But somebody's got to keep Jake quiet. Otherwise he'll give us all away. Please!"

Julie looked at him for a minute, then sighed. "Okay. But only because I promised Mr. MacPherson I'd look after him. And you make sure you're back when you say!" She hung on to Jake's collar as Kim crept towards the top of the hill.

As he reached level ground, Kim bent double and made his way toward the car. Crouching beside it, he listened intently. He thought he could hear faint music and talking. Stealthily he moved in the direction it was coming from. As he got nearer, he recognized the hectic exclamations of Eliot P. Jones, the disc jockey at CQVL, Queensville's rock station. Eliot P. always sounded as if he were announcing the invasion of Earth by green-tentacled monsters, instead of the number he was about to play.

Still crouching, Kim moved forward. He had no cover now; the trees and bushes had thinned to a few half-grown cottonwoods. There was still no sign of anyone — but Eliot was louder and more frantic. Kim bellied up the side of a small hillock and peered over the top — then pulled his head back like a turtle recoiling into its shell.

Not ten metres away, Claude Mallory was sprawled in front of a ramshackle cabin. Deaf to the blaring radio, he dozed with one hand resting on a pistol stuck in his jeans.

Chapter 20

Once again Kim inched up to the top of the knoll to take a look. Mallory's head lay heavily on his chest. A low snore, like the sound of tearing cardboard, issued in a ragged rhythm from his partly open mouth. Steve was probably inside the cabin, Kim figured. But how to get in without waking Mallory? Maybe there was a back door, or an open window.

Kim scuttled back the way he had come, and using what cover he could find, circled wide towards the rear of the shack. Once, out of the corner of his eye, he saw Mallory move and heard the scrape of a boot. His heart fluttered as he flattened to the ground and lay still. Thirty loud seconds ticked away on the watch next to his ear. He raised his head. Nothing had changed. Kim crept on until at last, just ahead of him, he could see the back of the shack.

It was a falling-down wreck. There was no door or window, but it hardly needed either. About a metre above

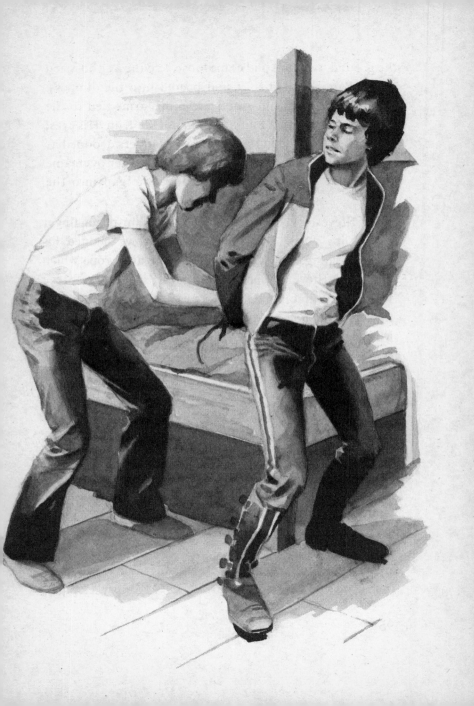

the ground, two logs had come loose, leaving a good-sized space. Kim sprinted to it. and peered into the dimness. Right in front of him stood Steve, his arms tied to the wooden endpost of a bunk. He did not see Kim. His eyes, half-closed, looked at the floor; his shoulders drooped as if he had long ago given up hope. Kim's anger overcame his caution and he slithered through the gap into the room.

As Steve looked up in amazement, Kim put a finger to his lips. "Ssh! Mallory's asleep!" Steve nodded his understanding. Quickly Kim untied the dirty rope which had held Steve prisoner for almost six hours. Steve wasted no time. Within seconds the two boys were through the hole and into the sheltering underbrush. Making a wide circle, they finally reached the top of the slope and tumbled the last few metres to the concealing foliage of the snowberry bushes where Julie and Jake were waiting.

Steve was ambushed by a wet tongue as Jake jumped all over his young master, his tail waving like a semaphore gone berserk. "Okay, Jake, okay! That's enough, boy!" Smiling, Steve grabbed the dog's insistent mouth. "Down, fella! Down!" Jake finally subsided in a panting heap on the ground.

Steve grinned at his two friends. "Okay, where did you three come from?"

Kim and Julie looked at each other for a moment, then Kim nodded for Julie to begin. "My story's simple,

Steve," she said. "Your dad asked me to look after Jake, 'cause he's out with the Mounties trying to find you. But Jake broke loose when he found your trail, so I followed him and met Kim here." She nodded at Kim. "Your turn."

Kim looked at the ground. "Well, I — I guess I did some thinking during the race — and I started to get worried about you. I mean — I knew you wouldn't miss the race unless — unless something real bad had happened . . . " Kim stopped, looked up at Steve, then shrugged and grinned. "So I pulled out at the bridge and came lookin' for you."

Steve's throat was stuck. He cleared it before he said, "You really wanted that trophy, Kim. You should've stayed in the race."

"Well, yeah, I wanted to win it all right. But like I said, I did a lot of thinkin' about stuff — y'know, about winning and losing and about friends — stuff like that." Kim looked away again. "Let's face it, Steve, I acted like a first-class crud and I'm sorry."

A silence enveloped them. In the midst of it the harsh rattling call of a belted kingfisher rose from the river below. Julie watched the emotions playing over Steve's face and his struggle to control them. Finally he spoke.

"Kim, it was my fault too. I did some thinking myself. I guess I came on pretty strong there for a while." He shook his head and sighed. "It's a heavy trip, bein' a hero!" He paused. "Uh, Kim — I'd sure like to be friends again!"

Quick tears blurred Julie's vision as she saw the two boys grin at one another. Abruptly she stood up and said, "Well, if you two are through with the soap-opera bit, maybe we could get the heck out of here?"

Kim and Steve leaped to their feet. "Yeah. Let's go!"

"Come on then. Our bikes are over by those rocks."

Steve started down the slope, then suddenly halted. "The Bobcat!" he groaned. "I forgot all about it!"

"You can't go back now," said Kim. "It's almost dark. Come on, let's get out of here! We'll find the search party and leave it up to them."

"We'll find them faster if I have the Bobcat," Steve replied firmly. "I'll be right back. Take Jake with you and go down to the bottom of the hill and wait for me. Mallory's probably still out of it anyway." He patted Jake's head, ruffling his ears, and said, "Go with Julie, boy, go with Julie!" The dog whined and sat down. "Please, Jake, that's a good dog!" begged Steve, half-laughing. Jake licked the boy's hand instead. Then, although it hurt, Steve made his tone stern and disapproving. "Jake! Go!"

The young dog looked at him. Finally, ears drooping, he turned away. Steve couldn't stand it. "I'll be right back," he whispered, then ran up the slope to the Bobcat.

Chapter 21

The sun had gone. The light lingering in the western sky was faint, thin, the colour of old bones. Steve couldn't see very well, but once he gained the top of the hill, he knew he just had to follow the trail. No way would he leave the Bobcat for Mallory to wreck! It was more than just a toy, more than a bike even. It had been a passport to the keenest pleasure Steve had ever known. He couldn't imagine abandoning the little bike — they had been through too much together.

He reached the top and peered into the dusk. No sign of Claude. If he never saw him again, it would be too soon, Steve thought wryly. Man, what a flaky character! And yet there had been a couple of times when he'd seemed almost human. Like when he'd asked if he'd been on TV, wanting to know what people thought of him. Or when that strange haunted look had come into his eyes as he talked about jail. Mallory had seemed almost normal then — although it was a pretty big "almost." Steve shook his head in pity. The guy was a real loser. But maybe he'd never had much of a chance . . .

Steve's thoughts froze as he heard a rustle ahead of him. He stopped and listened. No. Nothing.

It was now or never. Five metres away the Bobcat gleamed in the twilight. He crept up to it, and grasping the handlebars, turned it around and guided it noiselessly towards the ridge.

Then he heard it again — a hissing whisper of leaves and the crunch of branches breaking under a heavy tread. There *was* someone! Steve began to run, bull-dogging the bike along beside him. He *couldn't* get caught now, after Kim had risked his life to set him free. Fear spurred him on. Behind him he could hear Mallory's voice howling curses.

As the terrible sounds grew louder and louder, Steve panicked. Knowing only that he must get away, he leaped on the Bobcat and frantically kicked the starter. As he reached the crest of the hill, Mallory broke from the bush behind him. Two shots cracked out and flew past his ear with a stinging whine. Steve bent low over the handlebars and gunned the engine. Another shot sliced the twilight. Feverish with fright, Steve didn't see the root sticking up on the path ahead of him.

The front knobby hit it dead on. Steve soared over the handlebars like a stone from a slingshot. As he hit the ground three metres away, a huge explosion split the night. Steve lay still, shocked and bewildered. Then a piece of burning metal fell beside his leg. He looked at it, disbelieving, for several long moments. It was the new expansion chamber from the Bobcat, the one Pete had just put on for the race.

The Bobcat had blown up. One of crazy Mallory's bullets must have hit the reserve gas tank. The Bobcat was gone. Steve heard the words echo and re-echo in his mind, but he could not absorb them. He lay prostrate, unable to move, as flames crept from the smouldering metal and licked at a dead poplar. In seconds the tree was a torch.

A hundred metres away, at the bottom of the slope, Jake cringed and whimpered, pressing tight against Julie. His ears flattened to his head as one terrible noise followed another. A dim memory stirred of a far-off day when he had foraged in a barnyard for something to eat. That same dreadful thunder had pounded the air around him and had made a hurting fire race along his flank. Jake's tail sought a hiding-place under his trembling body, and he burrowed closer to Julie. With a long shivering howl he called despairingly to Steve.

When she was able to speak, Julie could only murmur, "Easy, boy, easy!" How could she comfort poor Jake when she was terrified herself? What had happened up there on the ridge? What had happened to Steve? The shots, the explosion — was he hurt? Was he dead? She turned to Kim. In the darkness, his white face loomed in front of her frightened eyes. "Kim!"

"It can't be! It just can't be!" Kim reached out awkwardly and put his arm around her. "Maybe Mallory missed! Maybe Steve got away before he started to shoot! Lots of things could have happened!"

But even as he spoke, pictures of Steve poured through his consciousness: Steve, lying in a pool of his own blood; Steve, ripped and mangled; Steve, dead. Silent tears coursed down Kim's cheeks.

Three kilometres away, Corporal Edwards, John MacPherson and Pete Sikorsky gazed in wonder as a geyser of yellow flame pierced the blackness, tossing clouds of sparks skyward. Edwards raced to the jeep and reached inside for the radio. Jabbing it with his thumb, he rasped out, "Delta One! Delta One! Come in, Delta One!"

The voice of the helicopter pilot responded immediately. "This is Delta One. I see the fire, Matt. It looks to be about twelve kilometres southwest. I'll check it out."

"Right. We'll make a ground approach. Keep in contact. Ten-four."

Corporal Edwards turned swiftly to the other two men. "Let's go! I don't know what's happening over there, but we'd better find out fast!"

Chapter 22

"Up, kid! On your feet!" Mallory snarled. Steve, still numb and dizzy, slowly sat up. "Come on! Move it!" The convict's boot caught Steve squarely in the back, knocking the breath out of him. Clumsily, painfully, he staggered to his feet.

"You didn't really think you'd get away, did you, you little punk?" sneered Mallory. "But how the hell did you get loose?" he demanded, jabbing Steve's side with the rifle butt. "Answer me, or I'll break you in two!"

Reckless with pain and fear, Steve yelled, "You really want to know, creep? I got a friend who came and untied me! And I would've got away too, except I came back for my bike. You better start worryin', though, I'm tellin ya, 'cause he's on his way to the cops. You're never gonna get out of here!"

Mallory chuckled softly. "Don't forget, Stevie baby — if I don't get out, neither do you. Besides, I know cops. Half of them are soft in the head. They got no guts. They wouldn't risk your life just to get me. I mean, what if it got in the papers? They gotta think of their public image, y'know! The press would have a ball with a story like that!" He poked Steve with the rifle again. "C'mon, kid, I said move! Back to the cabin!" Then he chuckled once more. "Yep, as long as I've got you I'm okay. Just think, Stevie, tomorrow you'll be vacationing in a beautiful little hideaway in Montana."

His brief anger spent, Steve stumbled through the underbrush. He had a terrible feeling that Mallory was right — they would be in Montana tomorrow. And he might never see Saskatchewan again. Boy, what a mess! He should never have gone back for the Bobcat. He could have made a clean getaway with Julie and Kim. What were they thinking now? After the gunshots and the Bobcat going up in flames, probably the worst. Steve wished there were some way he could let them know he was still alive. Then, with a lump in his throat, he remembered the Bobcat. His beautiful little bike — gone. Bent, twisted, strewn in burning bits and pieces all over the hill. Nothing left of it, nothing!

Just as they reached the cabin, a faint whirring beat cut through Steve's despair. What was it? It sounded familiar . . .

Suddenly Mallory stopped and swore, looking up. Steve followed his gaze. Two bright lights were moving towards them across the sky. A helicopter! The craft was almost directly over them, its powerful landing beams whitewashing the rough landscape with an eerie fluorescence.

His face hideous with rage and fear, Mallory stood in the glare, rifle raised, as the copter swung lazily above them like a giant dragonfly. Abruptly he put his finger on the trigger and fired, again and again. At the same time a string of curses, somehow more terrible than the bullets, spurted from his twisted mouth. Sickened and afraid, Steve felt the hair rise on the back of his neck — Mallory was insane!

He turned towards the boy and gave him a rough shove. "Get in! Get in the shack, you . . . " As the helicopter veered away in a steep banking climb to the south, Steve reeled through the door, tripping and bumping his head against the bunkpost. Crying out in pain, he sank to the ground as Mallory, delirious with anger, lashed his wrists to the bedframe.

Then Mallory's mood changed again. Chuckling to himself, he raced around the cabin assembling anything that would give light. He propped a flashlight by the door and set a match to the charred wick of a candle stub.

Spilling half the fuel, he filled a Coleman lamp with naphtha. As he pumped it up and lit it, he laughed and cried, "Light! Light! They want light, do they? I'll give them light!" He dashed from the window to the door in a frenzy, swinging the lantern, arcing the flashlight in wide and violent semi-circles. Then he picked up the rifle and fired a volley of shots into the darkness.

"Come and get me, pigs!" Claude Mallory screamed. "Hey, pigs! Come and get me! And bring a coffin for the boy!"

Chapter 23

The lap belt was too tight. The sergeant loosened it with a sigh and shifted his weight to ease the stiffness in his shoulders. Rubbing weary eyes, he put the binoculars down beside the seat and turned to his companion.

"It's Mallory, all right," Buckler shouted over the noise of the whirling rotor blades. "And he's got the MacPherson kid."

Dan Spicer, the best chopper jockey west of the Red River, nodded. His eyes hardened. "Should we go in?"

"Not yet!" Buckler pushed the radio button. "This is Delta One, Buckler speaking. This is Delta One. Come in, Thirty-three." He could see the lights of the ground searchers not a kilometre away.

"This is Thirty-three, Edwards speaking. Come in, Delta One."

"Hi, Matt, this is Bill Buckler from Queensville. I'm on the Mallory case and I followed a hunch when I heard the call for search-and-rescue. We had a report yesterday that Mallory was in the area. When I heard the MacPherson kid had disappeared I figured there might be a connection. There is. Mallory's got the boy — probably thinks he can make a deal with us — and they're holed up in a shack a couple of kilometres north of you." His eye caught by something below, Buckler paused a moment, then grabbed the binoculars. "Dan, turn on the landing lights, quick!" The ground beneath them was instantly bathed in brightness. Snared in the lens of his glasses were two small figures, their white faces looking up, and a dog. He spoke into the mike again. "Hey, Matt, are you looking for Julie Brennan and another kid too?"

"Yes, we are, Sergeant. Do you see them?"

"Yeah, they're right below the chopper, heading towards you. What the devil's been going on? Look, there's a clearing about three hundred metres west of you. We'll bring the bird down there. Meet us there. Ten-four."

"Ten-four."

A few minutes later, Corporal Edwards and the rest of the search party watched as the helicopter, bathed in the reflected glow of its landing lights, lowered itself to the ground. As it did so, Jake, Julie and Kim ran from the underbrush on the north side of the clearing.

"Dad! Dad!" yelled Kim. "Here we are!"

Within seconds the two groups were united in a hubbub of questions and explanations. Jake sniffed the air. It was crowded with friendly smells. First he raced to John MacPherson, then to Julie, to Pete, to Kim — and back again to John MacPherson. Puzzled, he sat back on his haunches. He had been sure his master would be among these humans. But Steve was not here. Jake stood up, testing the air once more. He moved slowly, muzzle close to the ground, along a worn trail leading back into the bush. Then his head lifted alertly and his tail wagged. With a bound, unseen by the others, he vanished.

The reunion was over. An air of grim determination reasserted itself. Kim and Julie kept close to Sergeant Buckler, resolved to be part of whatever was going to happen.

"Matt," they heard him say, "we'd better go in from both sides. How many men do you have?"

"Three, Sergeant. Gardner, Blake and Kowalchuk."

"Good. Blake and Kowalchuk can take the left approach, you and Gardner the right. Keep well covered. Mallory's dangerous as a wounded bear. I'm going to the top of the ridge and try to talk him into giving up the boy. Maybe he'll go for it. What time have you got?" The two men checked their watches. "Nine fifty-five? Good. Shouldn't take more than ten minutes. At ten-o-five I'll be in front of the cabin. Make sure you and your men are in position."

Buckler walked over to where Dan Spicer leaned against the helicopter. "Dan, I'll need your walkie-talkie and the bullhorn." The pilot handed the equipment to the big detective. "And I may need your help. Take off ten minutes from now and do a high hover above the shack until I signal you with my flashlight. Okay?"

Spicer touched his cap and climbed into the copter. "Right."

Almost unconsciously Buckler checked his gun, then started up the hill in long, loping strides. Behind him, in a determined parade, hurried John MacPherson, Al Chambers and Pete. Julie and Kim, unobserved, brought up the rear.

And alone on the ridge, a young dog lifted his head, sniffed the air for the hundredth time, then slowly crept towards the square of light where he knew Steve waited.

Chapter 24

Every muscle cramped with tension, Steve eyed his captor warily. Mallory's left leg now dragged noticeably as he paced to and fro in the tiny shack, causing his shadow, distorted by the light from the flickering candle, to lurch like a drunken ghost across the rotting logs. He was still mumbling to himself, but Steve could make out only the occasional savage curse.

Far above the shack, the chutter of the helicopter rose and fell. Steve leaned over as far as he could and peered out the window. Against the faint illumination of early night, he caught a glimpse of the craft's clumsy bulk. It looked oddly prehistoric — as if a colossal insect had been catapulted millions of years forward into the present.

Abruptly a shout echoed through the darkness.

"Mallory!" Steve recognized Sergeant Buckler's deep bass, made deeper still by the bullhorn at his mouth. "Mallory, this is Sergeant Buckler of the Queensville detachment. Come out with your hands up! You're surrounded!"

Steve, still leaning towards the window, felt his head yanked back as Mallory pushed him aside. His eyes glittering with a strange excitement, the convict sprayed bullets into the blackness.

"I got a kid in here, pig! A kid named Steve! If you wanna see him alive, you better do as I say!"

Behind him in the undergrowth Bill Buckler heard the muffled groan of John MacPherson, and an image of his own son, safe in his bed back in Queensville, flashed across his mind. He had to stall Mallory somehow, get him to bring the boy out into the open where they might stand a chance of rescuing him.

"What kind of deal are you thinking of, Mallory?" he shouted.

Claude Mallory chuckled in triumph as he turned to look at Steve. The cobra's crimson eyes rose and fell on his chest. "Hear that, Stevie baby?" he snorted with derision. "Didn't I tell ya? They wanna make a deal! Man, oh man, you are one valuable piece of property!" Good-naturedly he punched Steve in the arm. Then he turned back to the window, his face cold and business-like once again.

"Okay, Buckler, here's the situation," he yelled. "You get that chopper down in the clearing over to your left. Then I want the pilot to fly me and the boy to Montana, to a little place called Whitetail that's not too

112

far south of the border. Waitin' for us I want a car, gassed up and ready to go, and enough food to last us a couple days — and no cops! Got that? You get all that arranged, Buckler, then maybe we'll talk some more."

Suddenly Mallory's head snapped back. He had spotted two Mounties creeping towards the shack. Enraged, he yanked his pistol from the waistband of his jeans and squeezed off four shots in rapid succession. "Buckler!" he screamed. "Call off your bloodhounds or the boy gets it! Right now!" Steve shrank against the wooden upright.

Buckler was silent for a moment. He motioned to Edwards and Blake to hold their positions. Kowalchuk should be just about ready to make his move from behind the cabin . . . The detective took a deep breath and raised the bullhorn. "Mallory, how do we know you have the boy? We haven't seen any sign of him. I think you're bluffing! If you've got the kid, let's have a look at him."

Mallory shook his head. "Stupid, stupid fuzz. They think I'm snowin' them." He sighed. "Okay, kid, it's time for show-and-tell!" He laughed. "Now you'll know what it's like in a police line-up."

Quickly he took the rope from the boy's wrists and handed him the Coleman lantern. The mantle glowed with a searing brilliance. "Now, Stevie baby, you walk very slowly, very carefully to the door there and hold the lamp in front of you. Don't try any funny business like running away, because" — Mallory smiled and his voice took on a deadly tone — "I'm gonna be right behind you, kid. And I'll make sure you never run anywhere ever again!"

Blood thumping in his ears, Steve walked to the doorway on legs that seemed to belong to someone else. Framed in the oblong of light, he held the lantern in front of him as far as his arm could reach and let it swing for a minute in the strange silence. Through the thick leather of his jacket he could feel the cold barrel of the gun against his spine.

Then, faster than he could comprehend it, everything changed. A black and tawny shape flashed towards the cabin, fangs bared, a growl bursting from his taut throat. Jake had found Steve. Screaming a curse, Mallory tried to pull Steve close to act as a shield, but staggering backwards, Steve tripped over the fallen beam and tumbled to the floor as Jake, his forepaws like battering rams, smashed into Mallory's chest.

The lantern flew from the boy's grasp, its glass chimney shattering as it hit the floor. Suddenly a great whoosh of sound sucked at Steve's ears as huge orange flames blossomed. A shot whistled by his cheek, so close he could feel its hot passage. And then a series of bone-chilling yelps punctured the night.

Within seconds the dry, crumbling wood of the shack was alight and roaring. Black smoke rolled through the room. Struggling to his knees, Steve choked and gasped

for air. From outside he could hear muffled shouts as he shook his head and tried to stand. But his lungs seemed squeezed to the size of thimbles by the heavy layer of smoke, and he dropped to the floor again. He could see no sign of Jake or Mallory. He groped forward a short distance and stopped, all his bones gone soft. A furry body lay in front of him, limp, lifeless.

Jake! Steve reached out a trembling hand and touched the animal's head; the smooth fur in the tender spot between his ears was matted and sticky. Mallory had killed him! Mallory had shot and killed Jake!

As from faraway Steve heard his own voice screaming, "No! No!" Huge gasping sobs tore through him. Gathering Jake into his arms, Steve lurched through the doorway, now a fiery rectangle in the awful murk. With each gulping sob, he choked and fought for air. Fainting, heartbroken, he stumbled into the clearing.

All around him the night was filled with noise and flashing lights. The helicopter chuttered in to a landing, sending a brief hurricane through the underbrush. Steve's head swirled like a kaleidoscope as he saw Sergeant Buckler wrap a burly arm around Mallory's neck. Once again he looked into Mallory's wild and terrible eyes, and now he remembered when he had seen that look before: when Jake, caught in the trap, had so desperately wanted to be free.

Then the earth tilted and slowly rose to meet him.

Chapter 25

Everything was cool and soft and quiet. Wherever he was, Steve felt as if he could stay there forever. He took an experimental breath. Pure clear air — but with a puzzling tang. He opened his eyes. A doctor was bending over him, stethoscope dangling. At the foot of the stretcher stood his father.

"How did I end up here again?"

His father grinned, the tension leaving his face. "This time you came in by helicopter, son. How do you feel?"

"Okay, I guess," answered Steve. He couldn't get everything straight in his head. He remembered the fire, the awful smoke, trying to get out of the burning cabin . . .

The doctor leaned back and turned to Steve's father. "He'll be fine, Mr. MacPherson. Might feel a bit dizzy for a while, and his chest and throat will be sore for a day or two. But there's no real damage."

He turned to Steve again and smiled. "Well, Steve,

you can go home whenever you're ready. No sense taking up space here."

"Yeah, okay, thanks." Steve swung his legs off the stretcher and stepped down to the floor. His dad was there with a steadying arm, and they walked together to the waiting room. Steve saw Kim and Julie on the leather couch at the far end, with Pete and Sergeant Buckler. As they smiled and rose to greet him, to ask how he was, he suddenly remembered. Jake was gone! A wave of grief almost knocked him over and left in its wake a bleak and empty place. Jake was dead . . . Steve nodded and smiled mechanically at his friends, his head low, his steps unsure as he made his way to the exit.

Julie caught up with him at the door. She stole a look at him. Still looks pretty rough, she thought. Making her voice bright, she said, "Hey, Steve, great news! Remember the five hundred dollar reward for Mallory?"

"Yeah. So?"

"Well, Sergeant Buckler says we'll split it three ways, you, Kim and me." She paused. "Isn't that great?"

"Yeah. I guess." Steve's tone was flat, his face rigid.

Julie rushed on. "Well, Kim and I talked it over and we'd like you to have the whole five hundred so you can get a new mini-bike. Isn't that right, Kim?"

Kim caught up to his friends and joined in. "Yeah, Steve. You should be able to get an ST-90 with every accessory in the book!"

Steve stopped as the door swung shut behind them and tried to smile. He knew his friends were trying to make him feel better.

"Gee, thanks, you two. I — I think that's great. Maybe I don't sound as if I do, but — well, it'll really be great to have a new bike." His eyes were wet and he brushed a hand across them. "First the Bobcat blows up. Then Jake gets killed tryin' to save me . . . " He drew a shuddering sigh which ended in a sob and walked blindly towards the parking lot.

Julie and Kim looked at one another, bewildered. Then Julie ran after Steve's lonely figure. "Steve! Steve!" she shouted. "Jake isn't — "

She need not have shouted. Steve didn't hear her words. All he heard was the most wonderful sound in the world, a sound he thought he would never hear again: a cascade of barks ringing through the night as Jake, a bandage fitted to his head like a skull-cap, broke loose from Laura MacPherson's hand and ran towards him.